D0680638

Miss Charity Comes to Stay

MISS CHARITY

j C 7662 m

ILLUSTRATED BY LOUIS DARLING

COMES TO STAY

by Alberta Wilson Constant

THOMAS Y. CROWELL COMPANY   New York

This book is for my mother,
Marie Fite Erwin,
who never pioneered, but who, by precept
and example, taught her children that love
is the important thing in any family.

Chapter 1

I never in this world would have thought about writing a book if it hadn't been for Miss Charity. She said that all of us in Skiprock School were part of history. She said that anybody who came to the Cherokee Strip for the big run for land should put down all that he could remember because some day it would be important. That set me to thinking.

How would it be to write a book? I could see my name on the cover in big black letters. (Or maybe gold letters.) BETSY RICHARDSON. My real name is Elizabeth but it's too long for calling and Mama has to call me so much that I just about forget it's even my name.

If Miss Charity thought the run for land was important, maybe I should begin my book with that. The trouble was that I missed the start of it; I was down under the wagon with Rex, my dog. Tom—that's my brother—told me the Indians would steal Rex and eat him and I didn't know if he was telling the truth or just teasing me. Rex is part collie and part some other kinds. He can beg, shake hands, count to three by barking, and he can even drive up Old Blue, our cow. I have to go along to remind him what he's supposed to be doing when he gets to chasing rabbits but he's a wonderful dog and I didn't want anything to happen to him.

Our whole family came down from Kansas when the Cherokee Strip was opened for homestead claims in 1893. Some folks called it the Cherokee Outlet, but most of those that lived there called it the Strip—it got shortened, just the same as my name did. The Strip is that long, straight part of Oklahoma Territory that lies right south of the Kansas line. It belonged to the Cherokee Indians but they leased it to cattle ranchers, and finally the government bought it to open for settlement to those that were fast enough to get a claim and tough enough to live on it and prove up. (That last is really from Papa but I've heard him say it so often that I thought I thought of it.)

A lot of folks we knew in Kansas came down for the Run. Menfolks by themselves, mostly, but Mama said that the Richardsons were all in this together. It was a case of "united we stand," and we weren't even to talk about falling! Papa was the only one to ride in the Run because a person had to be twenty-one, or head of a family. Nell and Tom and I stayed in the wagon with Mama.

Now that I'm twelve (Nell's fifteen and Tom's thirteen) I wish I'd paid more attention to the way things were the day of the Run. I guess I was too excited. The riders lined up as far as you could see. Out in front of the line was a soldier, holding a gun. We could tell which rider was Papa by the red bandanna handkerchief he tied around the crown of his hat. Watching the line, it seemed like an awful long time ago that he'd kissed Mama and Nell and me and shaken hands with Tom and told him to look after the womenfolks. If anything happened to Papa . . . .

That was when Tom started to talk about Rex and how fat I kept him and what good stew he'd make. Most times Mama would have said, *"Tom, that will do."* She didn't even notice. Her eyes were glued on the line of riders, on Papa who was riding that show-off mare, Gypsy, and her hands were twisting a handkerchief to rags. Even Nell wouldn't pay me any mind. She was muttering, "Half a league, half a league, half a league onward. . . ." Nell thinks poetry will help anything.

It came over me that I couldn't stand to lose Papa

and Rex at the same time. I climbed down and Rex was under the wagon, lying in the dust. He put out his paw to shake hands and whined and held his face against mine. I was so glad to see him that I put my face right down into his ruff. I don't want to say whether I was crying or not, but my throat hurt, just the way it did when I had the quinsy. Anyway, I was there under the wagon when the gun cracked. There was a terrible roaring noise and the ground shook under me.

It was the Run!

Rex and I scrambled out from under the wagon. All we could see was a long, long cloud of dust, going faster and faster. Rex was barking, and I was jumping up and down, screaming. Not that I knew it! Nell told me later. Sometimes a wagon or a sulky or a buckboard would lock wheels with another and turn over and spill people out. In a few minutes the men on horseback began to pull away from the rest. I saw a flash of red going out of sight and I know it was Papa. I *know* it was. Quicker than I can tell about it the big wide prairie swallowed the riders, and only the heavy wagons, the men on foot, and the folks like us who were waiting were left.

I climbed back into the wagon, hauling Rex with me. For once, Mama didn't make me put him out. She hugged me and Rex along with me and said I must remember the Run the rest of my life. As if I could forget it!

Only, I didn't see the start.

It was awful hot that September. The dust was so bad it made breathing hard. Our water keg was empty and nobody wanted to leave to go get more so Mama bought some water from a man going up and down the line selling it. She told him it was a miserable thing to sell water and he'd never get any good out of money that came that way. The man got kind of mad and shook his dipper and said if Mama didn't want to buy water there were plenty that did. So she had to simmer down because all of us were thirsty. When her back was turned I gave some of my drink to Rex.

Well, that's what I remember about the Run. You can see right off that it's not like real history. I mean like Columbus getting the Queen of Spain to sell her jewelry, or the Pilgrims landing on a stern and rock-bound coast. If Nell were writing this book she'd put it all in fancy poetry and that might make it sound more important. Nell has a ledger that Papa gave her from the feed store back in Kansas. She writes her poems on the blank side of the pages. It's sure funny to read along about rosebuds, and Springtime, knights and ladies, and haunted castles in Nell's handwriting, and turn a page and there, in Papa's handwriting, is all about baled hay, shelled corn, bran, and shorts. But

Mama says that's the way life is, all mixed up. Furthermore, if she catches me reading Nell's book again without permission, she's going to give me a dose of peach tree tea. Only we don't have a peach tree big enough yet to pull a switch from so it'll have to be cottonwood tea.

It was about a year after the Run till we got our school and Miss Charity came down to be the teacher so the things that happened that day were dim and dusty in my mind. After Miss Charity started talking about how it was really history I got excited, remembering, and I raised my hand and asked her what, besides just the Run, was history, because I'd decided to write a book. She said for me to put down how things began, and for the Fourth Reader to turn, rise, pass.

It was plain as daylight that she meant for me to be quiet. Maybe I would have but Warren Espey turned around and put his thumbs in his ears and wiggled them to show he thought I was acting like a donkey. Well, I sure wasn't going to let old Warren think he could make me hush just because he's got curly hair and he asks for me at parties when we play Post Office. I put up my hand again. Miss Charity frowned. I snapped my fingers till she asked me what I wanted.

"One more question, Betsy. Only *one*."

"Do you mean I should put in about the beginning

of school and how Tyler Evans came to bring the black-board and—"

"We'll discuss this later," Miss Charity said, getting pink in the face. Everybody in Skiprock School knows Tyler's crazy about her and I didn't see why she had to act like it was some kind of a secret. The whole school snickered but I kept on.

"I want to start my book right now. If I start with Tyler—"

Miss Charity's pink turned into red. "Suppose you begin with your own experiences."

"I didn't see the start of the Run. Not the really actual start. I could tell about the grass snake. That happened before you came and Tyler was there and . . . ."

Miss Charity rapped with her pointer and when Miss Charity raps, well, we do whatever she raps about. So I hushed and the Fourth Reader began to read.

That was how I got started to writing this book. The things I put in it may not be *real history*—nobody would ever tell me just what was—but they're going to be true. Not about Princes and Princesses and Fairy Queens like Nell writes about. I guess I'm more for shelled corn and baled hay than I am for poetry.

Right off I found out one thing. It's hard to know where to start a book.

Authors don't have an easy time. We have a card

game of *Authors* and most of them have white beards
and worried-looking faces. I'm not figgering on a beard
but it may be that I'll turn out like Louisa May Alcott
who didn't even have time to get married.

Hard or not, I'm going ahead. Our copybook says,
"Where there's a will, there's a way." That means I've
got a head start because Papa says I'm the most willful
child he's ever seen and it must come from the Murdocks. That's Mama's side of the family.

Now that brings up another thing. My whole family
thinks it's funny for me to be writing a book. When
I told Mama she smiled in the way that means she's
smiling to keep from laughing. Then her smile turned
worried.

"Betsy, remember family affairs are never to be dis-
cussed in public."

"Yes ma'am," I said, quick as a mouse because I
didn't want her starting in to tell me just what-all I
mustn't write about. My goodness, if I didn't get to see
the start of the Run, and I can't write about family
affairs, and Miss Charity gets red in the face when I
talk about Tyler Evans—what's left? The weather's
not much fun. Besides, in the Strip about the time you
write down, "Bright and Fair today," you have to rub
that out and put in, "Blue Norther coming."

"I didn't mean to discourage you," Mama said.
"Why not get Nell to write some poems for you?"

That made me mad! I was going to write my book all by myself and no helpers.

"Nell's poems are about family affairs. After she wrote that one about 'The Fair-Faced Maid,' she wouldn't go out without her sunbonnet and she swiped a crock of buttermilk to bleach her face. And it wasn't a very good poem, either."

"I don't think you should say things like that, no matter if you think them."

"Why Mama, you said we should always tell the truth and shame the devil."

Mama threw up her hands, then she started to laugh. "Betsy, some days I don't know whether to switch you or hug you. Go on and write your book however you want to, but don't let me catch you putting chores off onto Nell on account of it. She's too easy-going as it is."

"I won't. I promise!" I hugged Mama so hard she said the bones in her corset creaked. I love to hug Mama because she smells so good. Sometimes it's violet soap smell, sometimes fresh-baked bread, sometimes the starch she puts in her dresses. But it's always Mama.

Still, I didn't have any place to start my book.

I thought and thought about it. When Rex and I went out to bring in Old Blue it was on my mind. In the Strip you can't just turn a cow out to graze because there aren't any fences yet, and the coyotes might chase her, or even wolves. We didn't have feed enough to

keep her up so every morning it was my chore to lead Old Blue to some good grass, and hobble her, and then go get her in the evening. Even with a hobble she could get quite a ways away and I'd hear her bell before I saw her. I went toward the bell sound calling "Soooooo boss, Soooooooo."

Old Blue was down in a hollow where the grass was thick. There she stood, chewing her cud, and watching me hunt her, just laughing at me. I sicked Rex onto her but before he got started he scooped up the trail of a jackrabbit and took off north. I had to run about a mile to round him up, then go back and get Old Blue and take off the hobble and put on her halter before I could start home. I was sure winded! Halfway home I topped a little rise and sat down to rest.

Rex came and sat beside me with his tongue out, panting. I get put out at Rex but I love him just the same. I leaned against him and I could hear his heart going thum . . . thum . . . thum . . . thum. The sun was slipping down the side of the sky and the shadows had turned blue. The wind that never stops in the Strip sighed past my ears. Rex's heartbeat and mine and the sigh of the wind were all part of the same thing . . . thum . . . thum . . . thum. I put my hand on the ground and felt the prairie throbbing, too.

There was a hawk riding the wind above us. He dived and came winging up in a curve so high he went out of sight. He was a part of the prairie, too, and so was the mouse, or whatever he dived for, that squeaked off to a safe place in the grass. "Everything's part of everything," I whispered into Rex's furry ear, but it was too big an idea to hold onto and it slipped away, even before I said it. All that stayed was the thum . . . thum . . . thum.

Straight ahead of us was our house. Papa and Tom were coming back from the field where they'd been working with the sod-buster plow to get the ground into shape for a wheat crop. Our team, Puss and Bess, walked ahead and the sound of the harness came in little jingles on the wind. Tom and Papa walked side by each and even this far off a person could see they belonged together. They walked the same way; they

pushed their hats back the same way. Mama came out to the well. The sun flashed on the tin bucket. I couldn't really hear the well rope creak as the bucket came up full, but I could *feel* it. Nell was out by the wire pen feeding the five hens and one rooster we'd managed to keep away from the coyotes. She came over by Mama, then they both went back into the soddy.

A soddy is what you call a sod-house in the Strip. It's made of sod "bricks." We had a sod roof, too, with the

grass side up so that from a ways off, the way I was, it wasn't like a separate thing at all . . . just a part of the prairie, a part of the wind and the whole wide world. All of a sudden I loved it so hard that I couldn't stand it! I jumped up and began to run. Rex ran alongside, barking like he was crazy, and Old Blue snorted and began to trot. I knew, I knew, I knew where to start my book! Right with the soddy! That was the place!

After Papa rode in the Run and staked his claim to the best hundred and sixty acres in the Cherokee Strip, he came back to get us and the wagon. I don't know just what I thought our claim was going to be like, but right at first it didn't look a whit different than the rest of the country. Not a whit! After we'd lived there awhile I think I'd have known any spot on it if I was dropped off one of those crazy flying machines folks talk about. Right at the first it was grass—nothing but grass.

There were the stakes Papa had set with his name cut into them, and there was the ragged-edge garden patch that he'd spaded up to show any late-comers that this claim was taken. And there was the tree. We were lucky; we had a tree. A cottonwood tree with leaves that twinkled in the sun and whispered to each other all night long. We camped under the tree and by the time we'd lived there for a week I felt as if I'd never lived any place else in my whole life . . . and I wouldn't have changed for anything.

It's not fair, though, to pretend that everybody felt the way I did. One lady that came clear out from Virginia cried and cried till her husband pulled up stakes and took her back home. Once they came by our claim on the way to town and she stopped the wagon and asked Mama if she could just come and put her hand on our tree. A fellow over by Hardpan gave his claim

to his brother-in-law *because he despised the fellow.*
Put it in writing! And Papa said that Asa Compton
just walked off and left his claim and shook the dust off
his feet. That'd be quite a shake, if you ask me, for the
dust that was raised by the Run never did settle down.
Of course there was Mrs. Merkle who said she wouldn't
live in the Strip if you gave her the whole six million
acres. She went back to Wichita. But that was after the
grass snake.

You can see that with no trees, or hardly any, we
couldn't build a house right off. We'd brought some
lumber down from Kansas, and a good thing, too, because lumber for sale was scarcer'n hen's teeth. Tom
says I ought to say scarcer'n hen's *false* teeth. No bricks
at all. So the only thing for us to do was to build a
soddy.

It isn't hard to build a soddy. Ours took about an
acre of heavy sod off our claim. Papa turned it with
the sod-buster plow that he'd traded the mare he rode
in the Run, Gypsy, for, plus a lot more to boot. Papa
was downright persnickety about getting the furrows
even. Then he took the spade and cut the sod into big
slabs. Tom did part of that and Nell and I got to cut a
few so we could say that we'd helped make our house.
Then we borrowed the loan of Ryman's go-devil and
hauled the sod up near to the tree where Mama wanted
the house. Papa thought it ought to be closer to Wildcat

Creek that sometimes ran and sometimes didn't, but Mama said that you could haul water but you couldn't haul shade.

Another thing they differed about was that Papa took a day and half a night to get the house true to the compass. He used a stake and a cord and the north star and he and Tom talked about angles and triangles and things that I thought were just in the back of the arithmetic book to make it hard. Mama didn't see what on earth difference it made if the house kept us warm and dry and had a place for the cookstove. She was getting downright tired of hanging over the campfire to cook meals and for goodness sakes, hurry up! Papa said he'd be a blue-nosed racoon if he'd live in a whopper-jawed house. It actually made him sick to his stomach not to know which way was north.

After that was settled we leveled up the floor and smoothed it off. Then we began to lay the sod "bricks." That was fun though it got kind of heavy after a little. You lay them just like building blocks, with every third layer turned crossways, and you use mud for mortar. I was the mortar mixer and Mama said she thought I'd found my true element at last and she was going to hire me out for a mud turtle.

The lumber we'd brought went into a frame for the house, something for the sod to lean against, and the two glass windows that came down from Kansas

wrapped in Gran'ma Murdock's goose-down comforter
were set in, one front and one back. Not many people
in the Strip had *two* windows, and some didn't have
any, just a rawhide door. The roof was hardest. The
ridgepole, and what boards were left from the frame,
and then tar paper—that was part of the boot in the
trade for Gypsy—and then more sod. A thin layer, grass
side out.

We whitewashed the walls and papered them with
newspapers. I think that's a good idea. Lots of times
washing dishes I'd read the papers on the wall and it
didn't seem nearly so tedious. I liked the advertise-
ments of Chief Snakeroot's Purified Panther Oil; there

was hardly anything it wouldn't cure. And there were the funny pictures that Papa put so much store by, the ones with Uncle Sam, and Mr. Money Bags, and one with horns and a tail called The Trusts, and the Donkey and the Elephant . . . all that. Mama put up a cheesecloth ceiling so that dirt wouldn't shower down on us all the time. All this fixing got us into the soddy before cold weather but the first time a big rain came Mama had to cook breakfast with her umbrella up, holding it over the stove. Water just poured in and everything had to be dragged outside to dry and we had to fix the roof in about a million places. "Live and learn," Mama said with her jaw set.

"Want to go back home?" Papa said, flipping a chunk of mud off the tea canister.

"Back home? I'm home right now and I'd thank you to remember it," Mama said.

"The Murdocks always were a stubborn outfit," Papa said.

"The only kind that could put up with the Richardsons," Mama fired back and before you could say zingalong, zangalong, boram, buck, we were laughing and the sun was out and the wind had dried out the wet stuff.

Our soddy had one big room, but we divided it up. The cookstove had the best place and the pipe went out the wall behind it. Next was the safe with the tin doors and the star punched in them where we kept our food and dishes and even the teapot with money—what there was. Mama and Papa had their bed up with a calico curtain across that end of the room and Mama's curly maple dresser was back of the curtain, too. Nell and Tom and I slept in a bunk—Tom on the top part and Nell and me on the bottom, curled up like spoons. In the middle of the room was the table where we ate and four boxes for chairs and Nell's little trunk for her to sit on. Mama's rocker was squeezed in, too, in case of company or sickness. We wanted the washstand but there just wasn't room so Papa made a little shelter by the door and we had a wash bench, like a ranch.

Now that I've written it all down for my book it sounds kind of skimpy. Back in Kansas we had eight rooms and a barn and a woodshed. Skimpy or not, we managed. Mama says that living in one room is a test of how much a family loves each other. She says anybody can get along in a palace where he can shut the door and sulk by himself but it takes real character to live with your elbows rubbing each other. Anyway, she reminded us about once a week, we weren't going to live in a sod house forever.

Shoot, I wouldn't have minded! Living in a soddy, I mean. There are some mighty nice things about a soddy. If something spills on the floor you just scrape it up and smooth it off. House cleaning means a bucket

of whitewash and a stack of newspapers. And a soddy's
warm in the winter and cool in summer. It can't burn
and it won't blow over in a tornado. That's more'n you
can say about a frame house!

There was one thing I did hate. It wasn't the fault
of the soddy but it came at the same time so I kind of
lump them together. That was gathering "cowslips."
We had to burn something, you know, and there wasn't
any wood to be had. In the old days they used buffalo
chips—I don't know why that sounds better—but what
we had were cow chips. There were lots of them, left
from the days when the Strip was one big cattle range.
Nell was the one that thought to call them "cowslips."
I guess they were about the only thing she didn't write
a poem about! She and I had the job of gathering 'em.
I guess we gathered a million. Two million. And it
seemed like every other one I picked up had a scorpion
or a thousand-legger hiding under it. First time that
happened I ran back to camp yelling. Mama turned me
around by the shoulders and pushed me right out again.

"We've come to the Strip to live and not let any
little old crawly worm scare us off. If we have to cook
with cowslips, we will. And be thankful there's plenty
of 'em."

I never got so I was thankful; I just quit fussing to
anybody but Nell, and she fussed worse than I did. The
first load of coal Papa hauled out from town we both

danced a jig around the wagon. Nell wrote a poem
about *that* called, "Bright Jewels of the Distant Mines."
I kept a shiny piece of coal in my treasure box for a
long time.

Here I've left one of the biggest parts of our life in
the Strip till now! Our neighbors. Our claim is close
to Rymans' and Gurdys' and Tyler Evans'. Rymans
are our very best neighbors. They came from Arkansas
and they have two twins. Not two children—two sets
of twins, boys and girls, in pairs. Believe me, when I
get married and have a family I'm going to have 'em
in twins. Jenny and Jeanie are thirteen—right between
Nell and me. They play the mandolin and they can
sing like mockingbirds. Shad and Thad are fifteen and
they look so much alike nobody but Mrs. Ryman can
tell them apart—and she can't all the time. On Sun-
days we go over to Rymans' or they come over to our
place. If we ever have any trouble Mrs. Ryman is there
with a pie in one hand and a dishrag in the other before
the dust settles.

Gurdys, now—that's a bay horse of another color.
Mama said we mustn't judge them; she says with their
start in life we might not be any better. But they *could*
wash! Papa says not to mind their washing, just hope
they'll keep their stock up. Their old mules broke
down the fence around our garden and ruined it! Just
ruined it! Tom's the only one with a good word to

say for Gurdys. Their boy, Garvery, is about his age,
and he knows everything there is to know about hunting and fishing and trapping. If Garvery ever went to
school it doesn't show. He hardly ever talks and his
hair hangs down in his eyes so that he looks kind of
like a squirrel peeking at you from the brush. Mr. and
Mrs. Gurdy look like the end of a hard winter! They
do a lot of fighting, too. She'll chase him around with
an iron skillet and then he'll go to town and get filled
up on red-eye and come home and try to shoot the heels
off her shoes. Honest! Of course Nell and I aren't supposed to know about that. Or Tom, either. I don't see
how we can keep *from* knowing things. Grownups act
as if children were the same as kittens . . . born with
their eyes shut.

"I don't figger Gurdys'll last," Papa said, when
Mama got to worrying that Tom was over there so
much. "The Strip'll take care of 'em. They'll move on.
Sod bustin' ain't what I'd call much fun."

" 'Ain't!' " Mama said. "And just when I've given
Tom a talking-to about the same thing. His language
gets worse and worse, hanging around with Garvery."

"Oh, he'll get shut of that in time. It's their ornery
laziness I hate for him to see. I went over in the middle
of the morning hoping Bill Gurdy'd have an extra
plow point and he was sittin' in the shade o' the soddy,
playin' a mouth organ."

"Oh, my heavenly days! Did he have one?"

"No, but I'm bound to say he offered to hitch up and drive in town and get me one. And he'd have done it, too, if I'd let him."

"Hmph! And come back full of fight and red-eye."

"Now, Louise, remember, they're our neighbors. When the gov'ment offered this homestead they didn't say a word about a select neighborhood. They left that up to us."

"There's nothing wrong with the neighborhood," Mama said, "except the Gurdys. If they'd just move off and some nice, refined, well-mannered—"

"That's a big order," Papa said, "but I'll see what I can do."

Tyler Evans was our other neighbor. He'd been a cowboy on the Circle Z ranch before the Run. Most of the other cowboys went to Texas, or someplace, but Tyler stayed on and took up a claim. He said he was going to make a go of homesteading, whether he liked it or not. He'd bet the gov'ment fourteen dollars . . . that's the claiming fee . . . that he wouldn't starve and nobody could say Tyler Evans walked out on a bet.

Tom thought Tyler hung the moon. Tyler let him fire his six-gun at a tin can and showed him how to throw a lasso. Then he'd squat on his heels for an hour at a time and tell Tom tales about the cattle drives. If Mama wasn't around Tom'd get him started on the outlaws that rode high, wide, and handsome with the U.S. Marshals after 'em. Tyler knew some of 'em, or said he did; anyway, he had Tom fooled a dozen ways to Sunday.

Tyler was so freckled he had freckles on top of freckles. He had red hair to go with the freckles and he was so tall that when he came into our soddy he had to be careful not to rake down the cheesecloth ceiling. He came a lot of times and Mama always asked him to stay and eat. He called Mama 'Miss Louise' and she liked it because she said it reminded her of the days when she was young and giddy and didn't have three children to set an example for. Tyler said if he could ever find another lady who could cook like Miss Louise he'd be willing to give up the joy of setting in on the bachelor's game of penny ante at the Diamond. Mama scolded him about that and told him he'd be better off to save his money. Tyler said he was willing to save a *lot* of money but to save on penny ante wasn't what you'd call real economical, considering what he saved on coal oil for his lamp the nights he went to the Diamond.

Papa liked Tyler, too, even if he did say the boy farmed too much of his time on horseback. Nell thought he was grand when he brought her the box of candy he won for being the homeliest man at the Thorny Hill pie supper.

That leaves me and though I don't like to go against my own family I thought Tyler was the aggravatingest, uppitiest, most . . . most. . . .

He teased me all the time and even if I am twelve years old I can't stand to be teased. Mama's talked to me, Gran'ma Murdock's talked to me, even Nell's talked to me, but I still get mad when I'm teased. One thing, Tyler always calls me Betsy Boy because he caught me riding straddle when I thought there wasn't anybody closer than Hardpan. He pulls my braids, and acts as if they weren't even attached to me. He beat me at croquet when I was the Red Rover. But the main reason I feel the way I do is on account of Miss Charity.

It's just as plain as the nose on your face that Tyler's stuck on Miss Charity. For all his talking about Mama's biscuits, he didn't even wait to find out if she could cook or not. One look at Miss Charity sitting behind the desk at Skiprock School and it was like the sun had come up behind his freckles. Maybe I didn't get in at the start of the Run, but I sure got in at the start of *that*. And I didn't like it. At first I pretended it wasn't true, even though I knew it was. I kind of hoped that if I pretended hard enough it would turn out that I'd made a big mistake in the first place. Maybe that sounds silly but it's the way I did.

You see, Miss Charity was the very first teacher we

ever had at Skiprock School and I didn't want her going off with Tyler Evans. Suppose he married her, and suppose he got tired homesteading . . . plenty of folks did . . . and took her off to Texas, and suppose I'd never see her again in all my life? Suppose some morning I'd walk into the schoolhouse and there'd be somebody else sitting behind her desk? Just to think about it made goosebumps on my arms the way a squeaky pencil on a slate does. No siree! Miss Charity belonged to us at Skiprock School and not to Tyler Evans, and I was going to do everything I could to keep them apart.

My goodness alive! Here I am telling you all these things about Miss Charity and Tyler when by rights you don't even know how she came to the Strip, or how we got a house big enough to hold her and us and have a parlor for Nell, or how I was un-skunked by . . . but I'm saving that last for a surprise. I guess I'd better back up and tell about the grass snake the way I meant to in the first place.

Chapter 2

On the claim we had lots of company. Anybody that stopped was invited to stay and eat with us. It's a long ways between places in the Strip and folks needed a rest and a meal and besides that we liked to have them. They'd bring us news about what was going on at Hardpan, or Enid, or Alva, or Woodward. Or the news from Guthrie, the capital of Oklahoma Territory. Or if they knew us and where we lived they might bring out the mail. Anyway, they were all welcome.

Papa always went out to meet folks, and he always said the same thing.

"Howdy! Howdy! Glad to see you. Come in and take potluck with us. If we can eat it every day it won't hurt you for one meal!"

Mama got so outdone hearing that that she threatened to give him potluck. Really, she knew that Papa thought she was the best cook in the Cherokee Strip and he only said what he did to keep from bragging.

Lots of times when there was nobody around except the family Papa would push his box back from the table, wipe his moustache, and say, "Children, take a look at your mother! Any woman with a storehouse full of vittles and a big kitchen and everything to do with can turn out a fair meal, but it takes a real cook to cook like your mother on a monkey stove in a soddy."

"Now Joe!" Mama's eyes crinkled, "you'll get me all flustered. I'm not half the cook my mother is."

"All due respect to Mrs. Murdock, Louise, but she has a heavy hand with lightbread and she can't touch your dried peach pies."

"It's the nutmeg. My father can't abide nutmeg and a dried peach pie without nutmeg has no more zip than a wet mop."

"It's the *knowing* that counts," Papa chucked Mama under the chin, "And the *doing*, too." After that Papa went off whistling and Mama flew into the dishes and spent the whole afternoon cooking up supper.

You may think that it's a long ways from dried peach

pies and Mama's cooking to the grass snake, b
wanted to put down what a good cook she i
you won't believe what Mrs. Merkle told all ...
Territory . . . that we lived on sowbelly and stewed
grass.

We first heard about Merkles from Rymans. Jenny
and Jeanie and Mrs. Ryman stopped by on their way
to gather wild greens and asked us to go along with
them. Mama wouldn't have it. She'd made up her
mind to houseclean and more'n that, she'd made up a
bucket of whitewash, so it had to be done. Still we
visited a while with them, standing out by their rig.

Mrs. Ryman heard from Stumpfs who heard from
Brunners that a Mr. Merkle was driving all around the
country looking for a place to put in a general store.
He had his wife with him because she was delicate and
he wanted to find out if the climate suited her.

"Well," Mama said, "if there's one thing we have
more of than any other it's climate. All kinds. Hot,
cold, wind, rain, snow, hail, and tornadoes."

"Don't forget that it's high and dry and that it's left
lots of homesteaders the same way," Mrs. Ryman said.

Folks in the Strip talked that way about the weather
all the time. As if they were kind of proud of how
aggravating it could be. But let an outsider say anything about our climate and they were down on 'em
like a duck on a June bug.

"Brunners said Stumpfs said Merkles were real rich," Jeanie put in.

"Not *real* rich, just *middlin'* rich," Jenny said.

"That may be talk," Mrs. Ryman said, "but I guess it's true that he's got spot cash." Mama and Mrs. Ryman sighed. Cash is rare in the Strip. Lots of people never saw twenty dollars silver from one year's end to the next. "Now come on girls; we'd better get along and let Louise get to work."

"Don't hurry off," Mama said, "I'm not so work brittle this morning. Keeping house in a soddy's . . . discouraging."

"I know what you mean," Mrs. Ryman said. "I made up dumplings to go with stewed rabbit and about the time I dished up, down came a clod of dirt. Right in the middle of the dumplings! Well, I served 'em anyway. Shad said he'd eaten his peck of dirt a'ready this month. Or was it Thad?"

"Shad," Jenny said.

"Thad," Jeanie said.

We got to laughing about that because nobody could tell the boys apart and Mrs. Ryman picked up the reins and drove off.

"Wouldn't it be wonderful to be rich, like those Merkles," Nell said.

Mama turned around like she was going to take a switch to Nell.

"Eleanor Mable Richardson! I'm ashamed of you. Money's nothing to get worked up about. I've known rich people who were trash, just plain trash. And I've known those as poor as Job's turkey to be the salt of the earth."

"Yes ma'am," Nell said, meek as Moses. Then after Mama went back in the soddy, her skirts swishing, Nell said, "I don't care; I'd like to be rich. I'm tired of being the salt of the earth. I'd like to be the sugar for awhile."

That was kind of surprising. Nell was the good one in our family. I mean she always did what she was told and never sassed back and hung up her clothes and washed her feet every night without being reminded.

"What would you do if you got rich?" I asked.

"For one thing I'd get us a house. A real house. Mama's just about worn out living in a soddy. And so am I."

"I never heard Mama say a thing like that."

"She never will, but just look at the way she works all the time and she can't keep things clean. There's nothing but dirt, dirt, dirt, when the house you live in's made of dirt. All our nice things from Kansas can't even be unpacked because there's no place to put 'em. We can't have comp'ny. . . ."

"Why, we have comp'ny all the time!"

"I mean if a boy, for instance, came to call on me, I couldn't entertain him in the parlor. There isn't any parlor. There isn't . . . anything."

"There is too! There's plenty of . . . of. . . . Anyway I don't know of any boys that are dyin' to call on you." I stuck out my tongue at Nell and ran off.

It wasn't really true, what I said. Shad Ryman was always shining up to Nell, and Grant Brunner, too. It was just that all this talk about having callers made me uneasy. If Nell was grown up enough for that kind of carrying on, well, I wasn't so very much younger. Pretty soon I'd be old enough. And suppose nobody came to call on me? Not that I *cared,* but just suppose! I picked up a clod and chunked it at Rex, not meaning to hit him, but he barked and Mama told me to get straight in the house and get to work.

I felt better doing something. I took the whitewash bucket and the brush and did the side walls in swooshy patterns. I got whitewash speckles all in my hair till I was a sight to behold.

A little past the middle of the morning Rymans came by our place again to leave us a mess of wild greens. They'd been over to a low spot on the prairie where Papa says there was likely a buffalo wallow in the old days. Greens came on faster there. Lamb's quarter, small dock, Indian lettuce, blue stem . . . I don't know what-all.

"Bless your hearts forever!" Mama said. "I was just wondering what I'd give my folks to eat. We're about out of everything and Joe won't stop his plowing to go after groceries."

"Bert's the same," Mrs. Ryman nodded. "He says we'll just have to live on beans and cornbread."

"Menfolks!"

"Can't live with 'em and can't live without 'em!"

Mama set me to washing the greens and picking them over. She put them on to cook with the very last piece of sidemeat we had. It was what Gurdys called "sowbelly." Mama had a fit if we ever said anything like that; she was very particular. She cut the sidemeat into two pieces, one to go with the greens and the other to slice and fry and make a little flour gravy.

"There!" she said, "Joe's certainly going to have to go to town tomorrow."

Nell and I were tickled pink! We started right off planning the trip. Mama kept in behind us, hurrying us to get things moved back into the soddy and straightened up for dinner. She said Papa couldn't abide a messed-up house but I think she was just laying it onto him. I think *she* was the one.

It was all done except for getting Mama's dresser back in and I was hauling on that when all of a sudden it moved—easy as pie. I looked around and there was Tyler Evans holding the other end of the dresser.

"Leggo, Betsy Boy. This is man's work."

I gritted my teeth. "I got this outdoors by myself and I'll get it inside the same way."

"What in the name of a Dominicker hen have you got on yore face?" Tyler said. "And yore hair?" he picked up one of my braids. "Pore old Betsy Boy's gone gray before her time." He gave my braid a yank, then he picked up the dresser and walked right into the soddy with it. He made me so mad!

"Howdy, Miss Louise," he said to Mama. "Here you've got yore spring cleanin' done and me with mine not started. Come to think of it, I never got my fall cleanin' done, neither."

"I don't know what I'm going to do," Mama said. "All this dirt!"

"Why ma'am," Tyler said, "I never saw any dirt 'round you. Thought it was plumb scared to light on your claim. Thought it blew right on past."

"Oh, you!" Mama shook her apron at Tyler. "I ought not to complain like this. I know Joe's doing the best he can. The poor fellow works from 'can see to can't see,' but I sometimes think he's forgotten all about getting a house for us. A real house."

"Nobody's got any lumber, Miss Louise. They've raised the price o' toothpicks till most folks've gone back to goose quills. I'm usin' cactus thorns, m'self."

Mama laughed. "You stay to eat with us, Tyler. You

always make me feel better. Can you make out on wild greens and cornbread?"

"I can make out on mud pies if you bake 'em, Miss Louise," Tyler said and took the waterbucket and went to fill it at the well.

"Mama, do you really mean you want to leave the soddy?" It was the first time I'd asked her that. It was the first time, really, I'd ever thought about it.

"It'd be the happiest day of my life to get into a real house," Mama said, "but don't you dare say that to Papa. Do you understand?"

"Yes ma'am, but—"

"Now Betsy, I don't have time to argue. You girls fly 'round while I stir up some cornbread and for goodness sake don't ask for second helpings. There's barely enough to get by on as it is."

I was standing there, staring at the wall I'd whitewashed, the one where I'd marked my initials in the soft clay that chinked the sod "bricks" and thinking that I didn't want to leave. No, not for any fancy kind of a house. Nell shoved me as she went past. Then we turned around toward the door. A rig had come up outside.

Papa and Tom were in the back of a light spring wagon and on the driver's seat was a couple dressed up, seven ways to Sunday. The man had on a tight black broadcloth suit and a tan derby and the lady—a skinny-

size lady—had on a brown and green changeable silk
trimmed with braid enough to rope a calf, and she
had a silk parasol held over her hat. I looked at Mama.

"I'll bet a million dollars that's Merkles!"

"Oh my land of love!"

We could hear Papa's voice booming out his speech
about 'potluck.' "Well, this time he's goin' to get it,
and no mistake," Mama said. But she straightened her
apron, pushed back her hair and walked right out with
a smile on her face. That was the way Mama did.

Nell and I looked at each other, then we both looked at the pot of greens. When I washed 'em I thought they were enough to feed an army. Now they looked mighty piddling. "Family hold back!" Nell said. Then she walked out after Mama, smiling too.

I sniffed at the pot liquor and wondered what we were going to do? It came to me in a flash. Greens were greens! On the top of our soddy there was a patch of new grass; I'd seen it when Papa boosted me up to patch a weak spot. I eased out the door, around to the back, and scrambled up on top of the soddy. Nobody was paying any attention to me. Tyler had left the waterbucket by the door and gone out to meet Merkles and all of them were talking. I grabbed with both hands till I got a lapful of nice tender young grass shoots. Then I shinnied down and soused 'em up and down in the waterbucket. I didn't have time to pick 'em over but you can't do everything. Then I slipped into the soddy and put them into the pot with the other greens and poured in some hot water to wilt 'em down. It looked like a lot of greens, now; in fact, it looked like a real plenty.

While Mrs. Merkle was admiring her hat—it was trimmed with grapes, roses, and two dead birds—and primping in Mama's mirror, Mama was stirring up some more cornbread and Nell was setting the table. Mama tried to introduce me but Mrs. Merkle was so busy talking about Wichita, Kansas, and how wonderful it was to live there, that she just jerked her chin and said, "Howdy-do, child," and I was half sorry I'd gone to so much trouble over the greens.

Papa put his head in at the door and called, "Dinner ready?"

"Joe's such a hearty eater," Mama said, straightening up from the oven. "It's a joy to cook for somebody who relishes his meals."

"I've always had a hired girl," Mrs. Merkle patted her false curls with fingers that sparkled. "Mr. Merkle doesn't want me to exert myself. Is help hard to get hereabouts?"

Mama stiffened a little bit. "We help each other when there's a real need but I don't know of anybody who works out."

"There's always help if you pay enough. *I* pay two dollars a week in Wichita."

That was more money than lots of folks made in a month in the Strip but Mama didn't bat an eye. "I'm sure it's well worth it. Betsy, set up the chairs."

Of course they weren't chairs; they were boxes and we called 'em chairs. That made 'em sit easier. But I had a feeling Mrs. Merkle wouldn't understand that.

Papa and Tom and Tyler washed at the wash bench. I guess Mr. Merkle thought he was clean enough already. He was telling all about the mistakes Grover

Cleveland made handling the Pullman strike. It didn't seem possible one man could make as many as that and still be the president.

We got squeezed up to the table and we had to wait forever and a day for Mr. Merkle to stop talking so that Papa could ask the blessing. Papa made it short because he said the Lord never meant for cold cornbread to take the place of piety. Mama started the pan of cornbread one way and the plate of fried side meat the other. When the plate of side meat got to Mr. Merkle he was talking about how much money he'd made in the cash grain market. He held the plate in one hand and took his fork and picked over the pieces, though goodness knows it was easy to see 'em all. He kept picking and talking and I saw Tom's nose twitch. He'd been helping Papa plow with the sod-buster plow and that's hard work and he was hungry. When Mr. Merkle finally stopped for breath, Tom spoke up.

"Thanks for the sowbelly."

The quiet was terrible. My face burned for Tom. He'd heard Garvery say "sowbelly" so often that it just slipped out. Tom gives me lots of trouble lots of ways but he's really *nice*. Really. Mama looked like she wanted to crawl under the table. It was Tyler who saved the day. Slick as a greased pig going under a fence he took the plate out of Mr. Merkle's hand and passed it to Tom.

"Was that there corn price shelled corn or in the ear?" he asked.

Mr. Merkle was off like a shot, talking about prices and money. Mama passed the greens to Mrs. Merkle.

"Wild greens are such a treat. My neighbor brought me these fresh picked this morning."

Mrs. Merkle dipped the big spoon down and lifted it up. I could see the grass string off the spoon and it was a different color. Mrs. Merkle's thin nose wiggled like a cottontail rabbit's. She lifted up a forkful of greens and tasted them. She chewed and she chewed, the way Old Blue does only Old Blue looks a lot pleasanter. After a little she made out she had to cough and put up her hand and when it came down she'd stopped chewing. Mr. Merkle was still off on prices, all about how he could buy wholesale in St. Louis and how he was going to carry the best lines in his store and sell for spot cash—no credit at all—and beat town prices all to smithereens. I tried the greens on my plate and they tasted fine; a mite tough but really fine.

Tyler kept looking at me, kind of funny. I made a little bitty snoot at him to show I hadn't forgotten that he'd taken the dresser out of my hands. Mama had only a smidge of lamb's quarter on her plate, put there to look as if she had the same as everybody. All the rest of the table were listening to Mr. Merkle; it was all they could do.

Then I saw something that nobody else did. The door to the soddy was propped open because the weather was warm, and to get a little more room inside. Around the chunk of rock we used for a prop I saw the neat, smooth head of a grass snake. It was early for grass snakes and this one poked his head in like he was looking for company. He'd slither a little closer and stop and wait, for all the world as if he heard every word Mr. Merkle had to say about Grover Cleveland's mistakes and how the Republicans could have done better.

Maybe I'd better explain about snakes right here. They were one crop we had a-plenty of! Big bad rattlers, blacksnakes, chicken snakes, blue racers, copperheads, bull snakes. The very sight of a snake upset Mama so that after Papa dug post holes for the pole corral and came back next day to set the poles and found a snake in every last hole—*every last one*—he said he'd pay to get 'em cleaned out. Two for a nickel. Tom went right to work and made his spending money that way. Nell wouldn't hardly kill a snake unless she just about stepped on it but I got to be right handy. Two for a nickel and no matter what kind adds up! I was on the last half of a two-fer, that's what we called 'em, and I hadn't seen a snake for quite a while so this was my big chance. The biggest thing to me was that with one more nickle I could get the patent-leather-

toed-yellow-silk-stitched slippers I'd seen in Hardpan.
My two-fer came sliding in the door, a yard long and
skinny. I crossed my knife and fork on my plate.

"Excuse me," I said, though nobody was listening.

Then I moved my box back, quiet as quiet, and tiptoed toward the door. I figured I could scare the two-fer
outdoors and catch him there, but you can't depend
on snakes! Like a blue racer he lit out for the table.
I dived but I wasn't quick enough. We both got under

the table in the tangle of legs and feet and shoes and somehow I grabbed at Mrs. Merkle's ankle and she screamed bloody murder. Right up against Tyler's boot that little old snake went, scareder than Mrs. Merkle. I grabbed him at the back of his head, and came out from under the table holding him.

"It's my two-fer!" I said.

Mrs. Merkle gave a yell that lifted the roof off the soddy a half inch. Then she fainted dead away. Honest,

you'd have thought that little old grass snake was a diamond-back rattler.

"Get that thing outa here!" Papa was yelling. Mama was trying to yank a feather out of the duster to burn under Mrs. Merkle's nose. Nell was crying. Tom was standing on his box yelling "sick 'em . . . sick 'em." The only one quiet was Mr. Merkle, sitting there with a forkful of greens halfway to his mouth.

Then Tyler grabbed me around the waist and carried me, kicking and squirming, out the door.

He took me clear down to the corral before he put me down. Down there he took out his handkerchief and mopped his face.

"Betsy Boy, you're pret'neart too much for me. Rather hog-tie a yearling any day. Now gimme that critter." I still had the snake, and he took it away from me and threw it in a long twisting curve. "Always get rid of the evidence! Now tell me what you were up to?"

I just sat down and began to bawl. All I'd been through to get that two-fer and probably I was going to get in bad trouble with Mama and now no snake, no money, no patent-leather-toed-yellow-silk-stitched slippers! When I quit, Tyler made me blow my nose and tell him about it.

"It was the last half of my two-fer," I said, "and no telling when I'll get another because we've just about got 'em cleaned out."

Tyler reached into his pocket and took out *two* nickles. Two! I thought he'd made a mistake. "Two snakes for a nickle; not two nickles for a snake. Not even rattlers."

"It was worth two," Tyler said. "The look on that old—that Miz Merkle's face! I wouldn'ta missed it!" He bent over like he had a bad stomach ache; then I saw he was laughing and trying not to make any noise. I laughed too standing there rubbing my two nickels together, but I couldn't really enjoy myself because of thinking what was waiting for me back at the soddy.

Mama came walking out by the side of Mrs. Merkle waving her bottle of smelling salts under Mrs. Merkle's nose with Mrs. Merkle shaking her head and pushing the bottle away. Papa was talking and waving his arms and trying, plain as anything, to get Merkles to go back into the soddy and finish dinner. Thank goodness, they wouldn't listen to him! So Papa yelled for Tom to go to the corral and get Merkles' horse. Out came Tom, grinning all over his face.

"Boy! Are you goin' to catch it! Boy-oh-boy!" That's all he'd say but he said it about a hundred times while he was hitching. Then he drove Merkles' rig up to the soddy with a big flourish and they climbed in and Mrs. Merkle put up her parasol like she was firing a shotgun. Then Papa yelled for me. Papa has a special way of calling; first his voice goes up, then it goes down.

"BetSY . . . BETsy . . . BetSY . . . BETsy. . . ."

"I guess I'd better be goin'," I looked at Tyler.

"Don't be in too big of a hurry. Joe's kind of upset. When folks get upset it's a kindness to leave 'em be."

"BetSY . . . BETsy . . . BetSY . . . BETsy. . . ."

"When Papa calls twice he means business. I'd better go." I started walking as slow as I could but I called back real fast, "I'm comin', Papa, I'm comin'."

Well, do you know what that hateful Mrs. Merkle did? She gave Mr. Merkle a jab in the ribs that I could see, clear from the pole corral, and he gave the horse a cut of the whip and they were gone in a cloud of dust, not even waiting for me to say "goodbye" or "I'm sorry," in case I was going to say it which I wasn't unless Mama made me. I call that pretty tacky!

"That clears things up some," Tyler said, "but I think I'd better take my own advice and mosey along. Tell Miss Louise I thank her for askin' me to dinner. And—uh—Betsy Boy. . . ."

"Huh?"

"Next time, take the sandburrs out of the greens." He got on his horse and rode off.

It seemed like a country mile from the corral to the house, and at the end of the walk was Papa, looking like a cyclone.

"Young lady," Papa said, "what have you got to say for yourself?"

That was when I got the surprise of my life.

Mama turned on Papa, her eyes sparking blue fire. "Edward Joseph Richardson, don't you dare start in on Betsy!"

Papa looked as if the prairie had cracked under his cowhide boots. "How's that?" he said. "How's that, Louise?"

"None of this would have happened if we'd had a house with a floor. No, and Tom wouldn't have said— said—'sowbelly' "—Mama nearly choked but she got it out—"if he had a school to go to instead of running wild. And Nell, here, almost a young lady and no place to have comp'ny. Oh Joe, I can't stand it any longer! I'd live the rest of my life in a soddy if it'd make you happy but I just won't have the children brought up this way!"

"But looka here," Papa said, "I was figgerin' on a deal for Merkles to buy out Gurdys. It's a good place for a store and it'd give you some pretty high-toned neighbors—"

"I wouldn't have that woman for a neighbor for a million dollars." Mama stamped her foot. "What I want is a house and a school and I mean to have 'em."

"Louise, I'd do anything on God's green earth to make you happy but there's just not enough lumber to be bought to build a house and not a schoolteacher that I know of, this side the Kansas line."

"Then we'll have to go back across the Kansas line and get one," Mama said. "And we've got to have a house to live in."

"By doggies, you're right!" Papa put his arm around Mama's shoulder. "I've had my nose to the grindstone gettin' things started till I've pret'neart lost sight of why we came to the Strip in the first place. I'll make tracks on some kind of a house deal and as for the school . . . there'll be us and Rymans, and Espeys and Brunners and Stumpfs and that new family, Stoners. And how about Garvery, Tom."

Tom scowled. "Me an' Garvery don't want no school. We ain't—"

"There!" Mama said, "you see, Joe?"

"I don't see why 'ain't' ain't as good as anything else," Tom said.

"You're right, Louise. He needs the three R's. I need him in the field but I'll make out. If I can just see my way clear to a house. . . ."

"A real house with a real parlor," Nell breathed. "Oh Papa!"

"How about you, Betsy? How're you votin'?" Papa asked.

I thought about the soddy that we'd made ourselves and how much I loved it; I thought about the place where our bunk is and how I'd made a little hole in the wall and put my candy prize ring in it; I thought about how safe the wall felt at night when I had a bad dream and put my hand out to find it. Then I thought about Mama. I didn't even have to took at her because I knew just how she was looking at me. Mama ought to have a house!

I put my hand into my pocket and there were the two nickels Tyler had given me. I held them out to Papa.

"That's for the first board of lumber," I said.

It was late at night and I was still awake. I couldn't keep from thinking about the soddy and how *it* would feel to have us all go off and leave it. I patted the wall and a tiny piece crumbled in my fingers. Would the soddy be glad to go back to the prairie again? To grow grass and tumbleweed and have rabbits running over it and quail nesting in it? The longer I thought about it the more it seemed right to me. I almost went to sleep but instead I climbed over Nell who sleeps like a log and I slipped over to the big bed. Papa was asleep; I could tell by his breathing. I thought Mama might be awake so I touched her arm.

"Betsy?" she said. Then she pulled me down and gave me a squeeze. "You'll like a real house; it's just getting used to the idea."

"I know," I said, "honestly, Mama, I do know. It's just . . . ."

I sat there on the edge of the bed a few minutes more. Then I said, "Mama, I put grass in with the greens. I thought it would help out."

"It did help out," Mama said. "It helped a lot. Now go back to sleep, Betsy."

Chapter 3

Breakfast was downright skimpy the next morning. Kaffir corn mush and that was all. Not even long sweetening. Mama and Papa had coffee made from toasted kaffir and some ground-up peabury coffee.

"I can stomach it," Papa said, "but I hope I don't ever get the habit because it tastes awful."

"Then we'd better get right into town to buy some groceries," Mama said. "And I've got a feeling you'll locate some lumber today."

"It'll take more'n just a feelin'. It'll take money."

"Joe, you promised."

"All right, I'm goin'. My word's out. Just don't try to rush me."

He took another swallow of coffee, made a face, and sent Tom out to hitch Puss and Bess to the wagon. Nell went out to see if there was anything in the garden we could take for trade. Mama put the sadirons on the stove to heat and told me to wash dishes and red up the house. Then she sat down at the table with Papa.

"I've got a feeling that Charity Whipple would make a good schoolteacher."

"Louise, you've got more feelin's than a centipede with corns."

"I haven't seen her since she was a little girl but she was quite bright and very pretty."

Papa got some ashes out of the stove, poured vinegar in 'em and began to polish the brass conchos for the teams' headstalls.

"I don't know about that 'real pretty' business. Could cause trouble."

Mama took one of the irons off the stove, wet her finger, and the iron hissed when she touched it. "I was considered pretty in my time. Don't know as it caused any trouble, unless you want to count marrying you."

"Louise! Sometimes you surprise me!"

"That's good!" Mama thumped the iron down on

the tail of Papa's shirt. "A man needs a little surprisin' when he's been married as long as you have."

That made me snicker and Mama went right on talking. "If little pitchers would keep their hands as busy as their ears we might get to Hardpan before noon."

"Yes ma'am." I scrubbed on the mush pot. "Are we really and truly goin' to have a school?"

"The Lord willin' an the creek don't rise," Papa said. "Your mama's got a notion that one of her kin-folks would make a teacher."

"Charity Whipple," Mama said. "Her mother was my second cousin Marcia, once removed, on my mother's side."

"I don't think we ought to get into all this too deep," Papa worried. "S'pose you ask her to come an' s'pose she says 'yes' an' s'pose we don't have any house to put her in? S'pose the neighbors don't take to the notion of gettin' up a school? S'pose. . . ."

"S'pose the sun don't come up tomorrow morning?" Mama thumped the iron. "If we s'posed all those things we'd never have got to the Strip in the first place. There comes a time when a person's got to step out on faith." She set the iron up on its heel and looked right at Papa. "I got up early this morning and wrote to Charity by candlelight and asked her to come. It's my intention to mail the letter in Hardpan this morning."

She pointed up to the clock shelf where we always put letters we've written to be mailed. There it was all addressed in Mama's neat handwriting. "Miss Charity Whipple, Care of Mrs. Egbert Whipple, Jourdan Bend, Kansas."

I read it out loud. Papa sucked in his breath through his moustache. "Betsy, go round up Tom and Nell and let's get started for town before your mama takes a notion to write the President to send a load of lumber to the Strip, right *now*."

" 'Twouldn't be a bad idea," Mama held up the ironed shirt. "If women had the vote the way they ought to . . . ."

"Run, Betsy, if she gets started on that we'll never make it!"

Our wagon was a green Studebaker that we bought new to come to the Strip. Papa drove, Mama sat by him, and Nell, Tom, and I sat in the back on folded-up quilts. Puss and Bess were our team, four-year-old matched grays. Mama said Papa thought more of them than he did his soul's salvation. Papa said that wasn't true, but a lot of a man's salvation showed up in the way he treated his team. This morning Tom had Puss and Bess curried and rubbed till their hides shone. Nell pulled some little branches off the cottonwood tree and fixed them in their headstalls. The brass fittings shone like gold. Puss and Bess liked it when we went to town;

they shook their manes, nickered to each other, and when Papa spoke they pricked up their ears and stepped high, just the way horses do at the Fair.

We always sang on our trips to town. Everybody got a chance to choose a song. I chose "Little Old Sod Shanty on the Plain." Then I wished I hadn't because in spite of deciding not to care, it made me feel choky to think about leaving our soddy.

Tom picked "Sam Bass." He always picks a song about outlaws. It worries Mama that he does but Papa says boys are *natural outlaws,* and it's better to let 'em sing it out than have it come out in other ways. Anyway, there's one place in the song of "Sam Bass" where we always get to laughing. It's when Papa sings out,

> *"Sam used to deal in race stock,*
> *One he called the Texas mare.*
> *He matched her in scrub races,*
> *And he TAKEN her to the Fair. . . ."*

Papa just booms out "he TAKEN" and Mama screws up her face as if she'd bit into a green persimmon. Nothing can make Papa change it to "took." He says he learned the song from a fellow that knew Sam Bass personally and, besides, it sings better without so much grammar.

Mama nearly always chooses a hymn because she says we get little enough religion without a regular

church. Today she picked, "There's a Wideness in
God's Mercy like the Wideness of the Sea." Driving
on the prairie makes a person think about the sea, even
if you've never really seen it. The long wavy green
grass changes color in the wind and the sky comes right
down to the edge of the world.

Papa chose "Flow Gently Sweet Afton." He says
Bobby Burns is the only poet he ever read who knew a
hayrake from a hairbrush. Nell picked "A Spanish
Cavalier," and pretended to play the piano on the tailgate of the wagon, making trills and runs the way that
silly old Miss Gerry Terryberry back in Kansas does.

After we got sung out we played "I Love My Love
with an A. . . ." When Nell got the "S" I waited to
see if she'd come out and say, "His name is Shad," but
she went on without letting on at all. "I love my love
with an S because he is Sweet; I hate him with an S
because he is Sassy; his name is Samuel. I'm going to
take him to Saskatchewan and feed him on Stew."

"Huh!" I said, "Samuel? How about Shad?"

"Maybe you mean Thad," Tom said.

"Betsy! Tom!" Mama warned us. "Suppose you take
'Y' and 'Z'." That sure hushed us up. It took me from
S to Z to think of things and I never did get a thing to
feed my love, Zachary, on except Zebra. By that time
we were in sight of Hardpan.

Hardpan's not much, I guess, if you come from a

place like Wichita. Mrs. Merkle said it was nothing
but a wide spot in the road. But we love to come to
Hardpan so who cares what she thinks! It has board
sidewalks, five stores, a blacksmith shop, a wagon yard,
a drugstore, and a school. It has two saloons but we're
not supposed to count them.

We hitched Puss and Bess in the shade of the tree
by McCurley's Drug Store and walked up to Merton's
General Store. Papa and Mr. Merton were friends back
in Kansas and both of them thought Sockless Jerry
Simpson who was Congressman from Kansas was the
big cheese. Mama said she'd have nothing to do with a
man with a name—even a nickname—like that. Papa
said it was a good thing women didn't have the vote or
we'd get a man in the White House named Algernon
Fauntleroy Vere de Vere.

Mr. Merton gave Nell and me coconut flags and
Tom a licorice whip. Tom and Nell laughed behind
his back at the way he treated them like little kids but
they ate the candy, just the same.

Tom ducked out to go down to the blacksmith shop.
He'd rather hang around, listening to the talk, there
than any place else in Hardpan. A man on the scout
has to have a horse, and a horse has to have horseshoes,
so a blacksmith shop's the best place to hear talk about
outlaws—and outlaws are Tom's meat.

Outlaws in the Strip were left over from the days of

cattle rustling, unfenced range, and having no Law
nearer than Judge Parker at Ft. Smith. Some of 'em,
Papa said, were men who'd been to the Civil War and
never quite got the gunpowder out of their systems.
You might live in the Strip a long time and never see
an outlaw; then again . . . . Well, it was that chance
that made lots of men carry guns wherever they went.
Tom and the other boys around Skiprock School
thought an outlaw by the name of Skip Rentner was
about the wildest, wooliest, toughest . . . they thought
he was just about *it*. Mama said she couldn't see why in
the world a boy that'd been brought up like Tom
would even be interested in that miserable kind of
trash. But I know. I mean I think I do. To tell the
truth, I'd like to catch a glimpse of Skip Rentner myself—from a safe place, I mean.

Mama was reading her list and Papa was talking
politics with Mr. Merton so I gave Nell our secret
sign, pull on the left braid, pull on the right braid. It
means, "Let's sneak."

We walked down the board sidewalk, looking in the
dusty windows. At Shaddid's Groc. & Merc. I saw the
patent-leather-toed-yellow-silk-stitched slippers! The
sign on them was $1.

They sure were pretty. I could just feel 'em on my
feet. Mama said they were foolish, extravagant, and
entirely unsuitable. Still, I wanted 'em. I knew exactly

how much money was tied up in my handkerchief, and
I knew it wasn't enough to buy the slippers. I kept on
standing, looking, the same way I poke my tongue at
a loose tooth—because it hurts good. Then, to be sure,
I untied my handkerchief and counted my money
again. There it was—ninety-five cents.

"How much?" Nell asked.

"Not enough."

"How much not enough?"

I had a notion to tell her to mind her own beeswax
but seeing the slippers had kind of taken the tuck out
of me.

"I've got ninety-five cents but a dime of that really
belongs to the church."

Back in Kansas we tithed our money. Mama said we ought to go right on doing that in the Strip but it was a lot harder to do. I mean with no church meeting regular I'd get to thinking it was all my money and not the church's. Actually only eight-five cents was mine to spend. I tied the dime up in a separate corner of my handkerchief.

All of a sudden Nell gave me a big hug and whispered, "For you, Betsy."

A nickel and a dime were rubbing together in my hand!

"But . . . Nell . . . you were saving up for that book from the *Youth's Companion*. Maybe I can pay you back."

"No," Nell said, "it's a Love Gift."

Gran'ma Murdock always makes Love Gifts to the church whenever she has something special to be thankful for. Tithing is expected but a Love Gift is extra.

"It's because of the house," Nell said, looking down at the board sidewalk. "I know you don't want to leave the soddy but you didn't put up any fuss because of Mama and . . . . Oh, go on and get your silly old slippers."

She gave me a push and I gave her a shove and we were right back to where we were most of the time. Only I had a nice feeling in my heart.

In Shaddid's Groc. & Merc. I was proud I didn't

have any holes in my stockings. I had darns but darns are honorable. Mama's darns are nice and smooth; not all bunchy the way Mrs. Ryman's are.

"Nice foot you got," Mr. Shaddid said. "Very narrow, high arch, nice foot." Mama said he was a sharp trader but I liked him. The slippers were a perfect fit! They came from St. Louis; it said so right on the box. Shoe boxes are almost as much fun as shoes, you can do so many things with them. I wiggled my toes, stood up to put my weight on the floor.

"I'll take 'em," I said, "cash on the barrelhead."

Somebody behind me laughed and I knew right away it was Tyler Evans. But I didn't care; that's what Papa said when he bought feed. I counted out my money into Mr. Shaddid's hand.

"Look at Betsy Boy gettin' all fancied up," Tyler said. "You fixin' to shine up to that curly-headed Espey boy I saw settin' with you at the Literary?"

I stamped my foot. "I hate that Warren Espey!"

"Betsy!" Nell said, all prunes and prisms. "Come back to Merton's with us, Tyler. Mama and Papa are over there. We were just going."

"I'm not. I'm goin' someplace else and you can't go."

"Now you just march right along with me," Nell said. "Mama doesn't want you stringin' around town by yourself." She makes me so mad when she talks like she was the boss of me!

"Come along, Betsy Boy," Tyler said. "I hear Merton's got sody pop on ice an' I'm buyin'."

I had a good mind to walk right off and show both of 'em but I don't get soda pop very often so I went along. I made a snoot at Tyler but he didn't notice so I wiped it off and pretended I was squinting at the sun.

Papa and Mama had finished trading and Tom was with them. Papa had a rolled up package with greasy spots on it and a sack that I knew had crackers in it. We were going to have cheese and crackers and bologna for lunch!

But first off I had to show Mama my slippers. I opened them and she closed her eyes and sighed and I could just about hear her count up to ten. Then she opened her eyes and said the slippers were very pretty and it was my money, after all, and she hoped they wouldn't "draw" my feet in the sun, and it looked like the only way children ever learned was by trial and error and I certainly was a trial! *And how about my tithing money?*

I certainly was glad that I could untie my handkerchief and show her my dime to give to the church! After that she smiled.

"Betsy, sometimes I think you're making progress. Now, Tyler, we were just going to the wagon to have a snack. Come along and join us."

Tyler went back of the counter and bought a bottle

of red soda pop for each one of us. Six bottles! Tom got out his fishing knife and opened them and they "popped" just wonderful. The best part was that they were cold and slippery from being right on the ice.

Ice came down to Hardpan from Kansas. Most of it went to the saloons but sometimes Mr. Merton would buy a cake from them. We didn't talk about where the ice came from for fear Mama would get the idea it was bad to drink pop that had been on ice that came from a saloon. Papa said that was splitting hairs too fine for him but Mama said she'd be willing to give up ice for the rest of her life to put saloons out of business. Mama was strong against saloons.

Tyler speared a piece of cheese with his knife. "Heard a little somethin' last night that might interest you folks. Blant Grubb's figgerin' on sellin' the old Diamond."

The Diamond Hotel had been there long before the Strip opened. Everybody knew it was a hangout for outlaws on the scout. It used to be a place for cowhands to come on cattle drives because it was near the ford of Wildcat Creek. Papa said it was wild and woolly and full of fleas; Mama said it was a sink of iniquity.

"That place!" Mama's eyes snapped. "It's high time the decent people of this community burnt it to the ground!"

"Why Miss Louise, I figgered you'd be interested in

makin' Grant an offer." I saw the twinkle in Tyler's eyes but Mama sure didn't.

"Buy that sink of iniquity?" A lady never raises her voice but I guess Mama forgot that. "You're making a very poor joke, Tyler!"

"No'm, I'm not jokin', just tippin' you off, kind of private. I got the word when I was sittin' in on a friendly game of 'Spit in the Ocean.' "

"Gambling! I thought better of you, Tyler."

"Playin' cards with Blant's not exactly gamblin'. From the time you cut the deck you c'n figger on gettin' whitewashed. But to get back to business . . . . Since the Strip was opened things have been downright puny at the old Diamond. Us nesters don't have much to spend on high livin'. Now word's goin' 'round that the railroad's gonna by-pass us. Blant's so down in the mouth he said he'd sell the place for a hundred dollars cash money. Lock, stock, an' barrel." Tyler held up his hand. " 'Barrel' is just a manner o' speakin' Miss Louise. I didn't mean you should run the bar."

"Well, I should hope not!"

"Blant don't own no land, only what part the Diamond stands on, so if Joe bought the place he could h'ist the house onto skids and haul it to your claim."

"By doggies! That's a good idea," Papa said. "But a hundred dollars . . . . Tyler, you know I haven't got that kind of money."

"Blant's a tradin' man. Give a little, take a little, you might get him down."

"I couldn't live in a place like the Diamond!" Mama spoke up. "I couldn't!"

" 'Twouldn't be the Diamond if we bought it. It would be our house."

"Skip Rentner shot it out with Blacky Adams at the Diamond," Tom breathed.

"We could have a parlor. A real parlor," Nell said.

"We could show old Mrs. Merkle if she ever comes back to the Strip," I said. "I bet a million dollars she never lived in a place like the Diamond."

"I'm sure she didn't." Mama raised her eyebrows.

"With lumber scarce as it is, looks like this is our best chance," Papa pulled at his moustache.

Mama looked around at all of us, then she put her hands up to her face. "I just can't do it. Please don't ask me to!"

"Louise," Papa said, real soft. "I thought you had more faith."

Mama took down her hands and looked at Papa. "Faith? Why Joe, what do you mean?"

"You said we ought to step out on faith and here the first time somethin' comes along you want to pass it up because it's not just what you fancy." Papa pulled his moustache. "The way I look at it, faith's a two-way road. You ask and you oughta be willin' to receive."

Mama shook her head, slow, like she was bothered. "A place like the Diamond that's been notorious for years. For us? For the children?"

"Like Tyler said, we're not carryin' on the business. I figger it's the folks inside a house that make it what it is."

"I guess I hadn't thought about it that way." Mama put her hand on Papa's arm. "If it's all right with you, Joe, it's all right with me."

Tom yelled like a Comanche. Nell grabbed Mama and I jumped up and down. If we were going to live any place besides the soddy I was glad it was the Diamond.

"Think what you're doin' for the neighborhood, too, Miss Louise," Tyler was grinning like a possum-cat. "Puttin' the Diamond out of business this-a-way."

"You men always stick together," Mama scolded. "I guess I'll never hear the last of this."

"First we've got to convince Blant Grubb," Papa said.

"I got a little money you're purely welcome to," Tyler said.

"Keep it in your poke, boy," Papa told him. "I've got me an idea. Get in the wagon and le's get started. I got my tradin' clothes on an' I'm ready to dicker."

"Hurry," Mama said, hustling us around, "but I want it understood that the very first one who throws this up to me has to write 'C-i-r-c-u-m-s-t-a-n-c-e-s a-l-t-e-r c-a-s-e-s' a hundred times in a copybook."

"So long," Tyler waved, then he brought his horse alongside. "When you get all that house-room, how about gettin' a pretty school ma'am I can take buggy-ridin'?"

"Should have known there was a catch in this," Mama called back. "First get your buggy, young man!"

"So long, Tyler. Thanky for the tip," Papa called.

Tyler reined his horse in a tight curve and held him to a prancing pivot. However I felt about Tyler—the big overgrown freckled-faced rapscallion—he could really ride a horse.

Papa says there's more history in the old Diamond than there is in most history books and it's a pity the walls can't talk. On account of that, I'm going to try to put down for my book just how it looked when we drove up.

To tell the truth, it was kind of disappointing. It was part log and part lumber, two-story in front with a lot of dinky sheds and stuff hanging on around. There were glass windows, mostly broken, and patched with all sorts of stuff. The front door was sagging on leather hinges. Nell said she thought there'd be flames shoot-ing out the window and Tom said he thought there'd be a dead man hanging in the yard, or anyway a Deputy U.S. Marshal. They were just making fun but I wasn't

joking about looking for the "sink of iniquity." My goodness, Mama always said there was one and they didn't need to laugh so hard when I asked about it. There wasn't any sink at all! Just a long wash bench with five tin pans and a roller towel that Mama said had been put up before the Run. The only sign of life was a broken-down bay horse standing, hipshot, at the hitching rack.

"Looks like business is off a mite," Papa said. "Well, that's all to the good for us." He hitched Puss and Bess next to the paint, pulled down his hat, pulled up his pants, cinched his belt a notch and walked right up to the front door.

"Boy!" Tom said, "Skip Rentner might be in there right this minute!"

"Well, if he is, your father can handle him," Mama snapped. The way Tom talked about outlaws always got her dander up.

Mama and Nell started right in to make the place over. Lace curtains at the windows. A parlor organ, after we get a crop. The horsehair sofa down from Kansas. Get Papa to build a plant stand out of that wash bench. I don't know what-all! I saw Tom easing over toward the corner of the Diamond so I slid over the tailgate and took after him. He gave me a look fit to curdle milk.

"Git!" he said. "Git! Or I'll cut off your ears and swallow you whole."

"You an' who else? Where you goin'?"

"That's for me to know an' you to find out." Then the piker called, "Mama, make Betsy leave me be."

Tattle-tale-tit, your tongue shall be split
And all the dogs in town shall have a little bit!

Mama didn't even look around. She just said, "Betsy, leave Tom alone."

I went back to the wagon. Mama and Nell were talk-

ing about a rag carpet for the parlor and wondering if
they couldn't get plant slips from Mrs. Ryman's Boston fern. It looked to me as if the old Diamond didn't
have a chance, once they got a-hold of it!

I leaned against the right front wheel and thought
about things. My new slippers. Picking strawberries
back in Kansas. The way a frog's tongue is hitched to
the front of his mouth. Then there wasn't anything
more to think about. I made lines in the dust and
played Tick-Tack-Toe with myself, but I cheated. So
I walked away after Tom.

Around back of the Diamond I found him, squatting
on his heels, talking to Mr. Runninghorse. Mr. Runninghorse is half Cheyenne and he lives not very far
from our place and he's lived there since a long time
before the Run. He wears long braids, like a regular
blanket Indian, but his eyes are gray. I know him just
as much as Tom does so I walked up and said hello and
how was Mrs. Runninghorse. Tom got riled up right
away.

"Can't I go anyplace without havin' you tag along?"

"It's a free country," I said.

"Mama said for you to stay by the wagon."

"She never said any such of a thing. She said . . ."

"Ne'mine," Mr. Runninghorse patted the ground
beside him. "Set an' make talk. Me'n Tom, we just
talkin' hoss. You talk, too, huh?"

"She don't know nothin' about nothin'," Tom growled.

"I do, too. I know . . . I know a riddle. It's a good one."

"This riddle? Like story?" I nodded. Mr. Running-horse's gray eyes smiled. "In old days my people tell stories. Set in lodge—one tell story—next one tie story onto it. All night tell story."

"I got this one out of a book."

"Sufferin' snakes," Tom groaned.

"This is the way it goes. 'Constantinople is a very hard word. Can you spell it?'" I had a feeling that Mr. Runninghorse hadn't heard me so I said it again, louder, and slower. "Con-stan-ti-no-ple is a very hard word."

"Sufferin' snakes, everybody in the world knows that."

Mr. Runninghorse was frowning, shaking his head. This time I yelled. *"Constantinople is a very hard word."*

"That's right. Very hard word." He settled back and took out his pipe. He wasn't a bit bothered, but I was.

"It's the 'it' that's the riddle part. It's the 'it'."

"For Pete's sake," Tom said, "don't pay her any mind. Go on and tell about the old days."

"You tell my girl," Mr. Runninghorse said to me. "She been to school. She tell me." He rubbed a handful of tobacco between his palms, stuffed it into his pipe and lighted it. Smoke came in little streams from the corners of his mouth. I wish I could do that. I tried it once with Gran'pa Murdock's pipe but I'll never try it again. Double never!

Mr. Runninghorse looked over at Tom.

"You like the old days, huh?"

"Yeah. Better'n now. Did you—did you ever see a real outlaw?"

"Sure. In the old days they come through all time. Stop off. Eat good. Sleep good. Take good horse, leave bad horse." Mr. Runninghorse's gray eyes crinkled. "You like that if it happen at your lodge?"

"Well," Tom said, "I—I dunno. Anyway, I wisht I could see one. I wisht I could see Skip Rentner."

Mr. Runninghorse shook his head and the little streams of smoke came faster. "That Skip . . . he draws gun like lightnin' strikes." He made a zig-zag with his long brown finger and I could see lightning in the sky.

"You think he'll ever come thisaway again?"

Mr. Runninghorse's shoulders moved. "Who knows lightnin'? Maybeso he come. Maybeso he stays 'way. If he comes it'll be to the Diamond. He left his mark on it. You see Skip's mark?"

"Naw," Tom said, "I never been inside."

"Mama would have a double duck conniption fit if

he went in the Diamond," I said. "She'd give him Hail
Columbia, Happy Land!"

"Aw, be quiet," Tom said. "I'm no baby. I just happen not to've been inside the Diamond. That's all."

"You come 'long with me," Mr. Runninghorse said.
He walked us over to a window that was stuffed with
an old hat. He pulled out the hat and we looked inside.
It was dim and hard to see much. In the corner where
he pointed I could see a hole in the log wall and the
chinking gone above it.

"Blacky Adams, he was standin' right there, when
Skip Rentner came up. They'd had trouble. Maybeso
girl . . . money . . . horse . . . . Blacky drew his
gun but he didn't have no chance." He made the
lightning sign again. "Skip's bullet hit Blacky, then it
hit wall. Skip say leave it there. It was his mark—like
cattle brand. I saw it all from under that table." Mr.
Runninghorse grinned at the way Tom looked. "That's
best place for Indian when white men shoot."

"But you're half white man."

"That's right, but smart half's Indian. Come 'long."

But Tom didn't leave. He just kept on staring in
the window at that hole in the wall till Mama called
us both.

"Where have you two been?" Mama said, but she
didn't want to know. She was looking over our heads
at the front door of the Diamond. "Not a sound out

of your papa in all this time. You don't suppose that awful Blant Grubb . . ."

"Papa's all right," Tom said. "Mama, we've gotta have this house. We've just plain gotta."

"The way you talk I think we'd better work on a school before we do a house."

"School? Who cares about old school? Mama, do you know, do you reelize there's a bullet hole in the wall in there that Skip Rentner put through Blacky Adams? Right in the very wall and Skip said it was his mark and Jess Runninghorse said he'd come back—" I nudged him in the ribs. Tom's older than I am but he hasn't figgered out yet what'll put Mama on the warpath.

"I suppose we can get the hole filled in," Mama said.

"But, Mama—"

"I can tell you right now there'll be no bullet holes in our house if I can help it. And no more loose talk about your precious Skip Rentner. Thank goodness! There's Joe!"

Papa came out and a little tubby man was with him. He had a bald head that he kept polishing with a red handkerchief. Someway he didn't fit with the stories about the old Diamond, any more than the house looked the way I thought it would. Papa introduced him to Mama and she was stiff but polite. He didn't say a thing about us, so I knew this was one of the times that Papa believed children should be seen and not heard.

Mr. Grubb walked around the wagon and came up to Puss and smacked her on the withers. Puss is the skittish one. She jerked her head and started to back and that turned Bess spooky. No telling what would have happened if Mama hadn't got the reins.

"Thought you said they was gentle," Mr. Grubb said.

"Didn't figger you wanted rockin' horses," Papa said.

"Hmmmmm," Mr. Grubb switched his toothpick around in his mouth. He walked around the team, made Bess open her mouth. Rocked back and forth on his heels a few times. "It's a deal," he said. "I'll git 'em soon as the house's moved."

"Soon as it's moved," Papa said, "an' there's not a better team in the Strip."

"Joe!" Mama put her hand to her mouth. "I won't let you!"

" 'Scuse me." Papa said to Mr. Grubb. "It's the only thing we've got to trade with, Louise. It's Puss and Bess or it's no house."

There were white lines around Papa's mouth, just the way there were when he thought Tom had blood poisoning.

"But Puss and Bess—why they're like part of the family. You raised 'em, Joe. I can't ask it of you."

"It's my deal," Papa said. There was a crooked grin on his face that slipped a little but he got it back on. "I guess I got to do a little steppin' out on faith myself."

Then he turned around and shook hands with Blant Grubb and jerked his head at us to get into the wagon. I guess we'd gone a half mile before anybody made a sound. The way I felt . . . . Well, I just can't tell about it. Then Mama took a deep breath and began to sing:

> *How firm a foundation, ye saints of the Lord,*
> *Is built on our faith in His excellent word. . . .*

Tears were streaking down Mama's face but she kept singing and pretty soon Papa joined in, then all the rest of us and we sang all the way back to the claim.

Chapter 4

*T*hat was the craziest summer!

Putting it all down for my book makes it neat and connected. Really, it was like the magic lantern show at Skiprock School. The pictures all red and blue and green but all of different things.

Papa started right in getting things rounded up for the moving. First off, he and Tom took a whole day just walking around the Diamond, figgering. Skids wouldn't do it, the way Tyler said; it was going to take timbers and screw jacks. Papa groaned. Likely there weren't enough in the whole Strip.

Mama put her hands on her hips. "Now Joe, I'm willing to do anything or do without anything to get this house. Just don't say it can't be done."

"Yes ma'am," Papa said, "but where'm I gonna get timbers . . . ?"

"Work for the night is coming. . . ." Mama began to sing real loud. Papa left.

The days went along and he still couldn't find any timbers. Big logs, I mean, to use for rollers under the Diamond. It was the same old trouble . . . no trees in the country. Once I caught Papa walking around our big cottonwood with Mama's tape line in his hand. I almost died! Cut down our only tree!

"Papa! I'd rather live in the soddy the rest of my life! You wouldn't!"

"Betsy, get the 'woodsman spare that tree' look out of your eyes. I'm just trying to figger. Cottonwood's no good for work like this. Too soft."

The jacks weren't so hard to find. Papa had five located when he heard that Mr. Ed Brunner had an extra good one his father had brought from Germany. He went over and asked for the loan of it and do you know what? Mr. Brunner said he could *hire* it.

"I'd rather die in the poorhouse than act like some people," Mama said.

"I don't care what they act like if they've got the tools," Papa said, "I tell you, Louise, this thing's about got me whipped. If I could just get timbers—"

There are lots of special ways to get things you want real bad. Nell wishes on the first star every evening.

"Starlight, star bright, very first star I've seen tonight." Jennie and Jeanie Ryman think red birds are better. I've always had best luck stamping white horses. Every time you see one lick your finger, touch the palm of your other hand, and then "stamp" the spot you've touched with your doubled-up fist. When you've stamped a hundred you get your wish. I got my trip to Wichita that way when I was only eight years old. I've got other things, too, but I can't think of 'em right now and Mama always says I was going to get them anyway, but Papa says if a thing makes you feel lucky it's all to the good.

Well, I'd been stamping white horses to get a Victoria Safety Bicycle with a Tilting Saddle, like Maude Ames had back in Kansas, when I decided to change over to some timbers for Papa. After all a bicycle on the claim wouldn't do much good. The very day I changed over I saw three white horses pass our place! It wasn't any time at all till I got my hundred.

So I wasn't a bit surprised when a scrawny little man in rag-tag clothes came up to our house and asked if Papa was the one that wanted some timbers. They stood talking, quite a while, and I couldn't hear what they were saying because I had to hold Rex. He was barking at the little man till you'd have thought he was going to eat him, torn hat, patched overalls and all.

Papa and the little man went away together. When

they came back they were walking alongside the skin-
niest yoke of oxen I ever saw in my life. Their ribs
were like washboards. On a sledge behind them were
four big cedar logs.

I yelled for Mama and ran to meet them.

"Where'd you ever find such big trees?" As soon as
I said it I knew that I oughtn't to've.

"Don't be so nosy," Mama said, coming up behind
me.

"I sure never saw any trees like that around here.
Even in Kansas—"

"Well, Sis," the little man wheezed, "I got them
timbers off'n Section Thirty-Seven, you might say."

Anybody who's lived in the Cherokee Strip as much
as fifteen minutes knows the land is divided up into
sections and they're numbered one to thirty-six. Then
the numbers start over. Section Thirty-Seven just
wasn't anywhere. I had my mouth open to say as much
when Mama gave me her Close-It-Quick look.

After the timbers were unloaded and the little man
was clear out of sight I couldn't help asking, "Where
is Section Thirty-Seven, Papa? Where?"

He didn't say a word so I thought he didn't hear me
and I asked again.

"Tell her, Joe," Mama said, "she'll never give you
a minute's peace."

Papa wiped his face with his bandana handkerchief.

"All right, Betsy, if you've *got* to know. There's no such place as Section Thirty-Seven. It's just an easier thing than to come right out and say the timber was stole off the gover'ment reservation."

"You mean that little man was a—thief?"

"No more'n what I am if it comes to that. I knew where he got the logs."

"Now Joe," Mama said, "you only bought it; you didn't cut it."

"I say I'm tarred with the same brush," Papa said. "But, by doggies, it looks like the gover'ment makes it hard to be honest. All those rules—"

"They've got to have rules," Mama said.

"Sure, but a man's got to have victuals. Take that feller—got a homestead over by Woodward, six kids to get through till grass, scrapin' the bottom of the meal sack, well caved in, cow got Texas fever—who's to blame him for cuttin' some timber that don't look like it b'longs to nobody?" Papa kicked the near log. "Anybody goes to jail it oughta be me."

To think about Papa in jail—that nasty little box in Hardpan—made me sick and cold and hot and mad at the same time. I grabbed him around the waist. "I won't let them take you to jail! I won't!"

Papa took my arms loose. "Nobody's goin' to jail. It's just—well, a man don't like to admit he's done wrong; not even if he thinks it's right."

"It was my fault, too," I said; "I stamped white horses."

"Good for you," Papa said, "now go get Tom and tell him to hook up Puss and Bess and we'll take these timbers over to the Diamond."

The way they did was to knock holes in the foundation and run the timbers through. Then with the jacks —Mr. Brunner's, too—they lifted the house and knocked out the rest of the foundation and let the house down, easy, EEEEEEEEasy, till it rested on the timbers that were rollers now. Papa and Tom worked every day. Lots of others helped when they could. Tyler Evans and Mr. Ryman helped the most. Sometimes Mr. Gurdy or Mr. Brunner came.

"Is Al Brunner working for hire?" Mama wanted to know.

"Nope. For free," Papa grinned. "As long as I let him give out advice."

"Is he a good hand?"

"Oh he's a top hand at working. I'm not sure how you'll like his advice. He wants me to close off that room you picked for the parlor and store hay in it."

"Papa!"

Honestly, I thought Nell had run a nail in her foot!

"Nell, you ought to know your father better'n that," Mama said. "Joe, I won't have you teasing the child."

"I never said I *took* his advice," Papa said. "I just said he *gave* it."

Espeys helped, too. Mr. Espey and Warren. I ought to know! Tyler teased me about Warren till I threw a bucket of water at him. Then Mama made me apologize. I said I was sorry but under my breath I said, "Sorry it wasn't a bucket of mud."

At last the day came when the Diamond was ready to roll. Papa had two teams spoken for besides Puss and Bess. Rymans' Buck and Sandy, and Espeys' Jake and Jeems. Jeems was a mouse-colored mule and mean as all get out. Warren had to come along because he was the only one that could get Jeems out of a balk. Papa said a house-moving job was no place for women and children and Nell and I were to stay home with Mama. The middle of the morning she weakened and let us go watch with Jenny and Jeanie.

They came by in the buckboard and Mama stood out there telling us, "Behave like ladies. . . . Do just what Papa says. . . . Don't bother the menfolks. . . . Stay away from the horses. . . ." And about a million more things.

I wanted to get there at the start, remembering that I'd missed the start of the Run. I tell you I "pushed" that buckboard and that broken-down horse of Rymans till I was worn out. It didn't do a bit of good! I

didn't even get first sight. It was Jenny that squealed, "Looky! Looky! Looky!"

There came the Diamond, trundling up the road. The porch was gone and the one-story shed. All the window glass that wasn't broken already had been taken out. It made the house look like an old man that's lost his glasses, staring and staring. I felt kind of sorry for the house and I wished I could tell it that things would be better when it got settled on the claim.

First, Papa would start Puss and Bess, then the other teams would fall in and the traces would pull out straight and the house would move ahead on the rollers, creaking and groaning and complaining. When the backmost roller got to the end of the house they'd snake it out, run it under the front, and start the teams again. I thought Papa was pretty smart to figger out all of that, but he said, land o' love, it was as old as the pyramids—maybe it was the way they built the pyramids, for all he knew. It worked, but you can see for yourself that it was as slow as the seven-year itch.

There was plenty of time to get out from underfoot when the teams started and we girls kept edging up closer and closer. Papa would notice and yell, "You girls! Git back!" And we'd move back; then we'd move up again. In between hitches Warren Espey would come over and talk to us.

"He's cute," Jeanie said when he'd gone back to start Jeems.

"Cute means bowlegged," I said.

"If you don't want him, I'll take him when he grows up," Jenny giggled.

I knew she was only joking—she's crazy about Trib Carter—but my face got hot and the three of them laughed at me till they almost had the rolling fits. Silly! I hope I never act like that when I get to be a big girl.

Tyler rode home with Papa and Tom that night and he brought me a horsehair ring Warren made from hairs out of Jake's tail. I threw it away, but I saw where it landed and after Tyler left I went out and found it.

The first day they made a mile.

We found out later that a mile was a real good day. Some days they didn't make a quarter-mile. Some days the Rymans or the Espeys had to use their teams themselves. Then there was Sunday. And the day Mr. Gurdy had been hitting the jug and he fell off the top of the Diamond. Mama said it was a judgment on him but Papa said a fall like that would have killed a sober man and Gurdy wasn't hurt a bit.

I got the feeling that the moving would go on and on and we'd never have to leave the soddy. It was a jolt when Papa said, "Next Sat'day we'll have 'er in place."

"Oh Joe! Our house!" Mama hugged him and I hugged her and Nell hugged me and Tom said we looked like a batch of fishworms.

"Now girls, we've got to make plans," Mama said in the voice that means we're in for a lot of work and we'd better not try to get out of it. "We want to do something special for all the folks that've helped us get our house."

The next two days Mama cooked. She no more'n got one thing done than she started another. Nell helped and so did Mrs. Ryman and I washed dishes. I bet I washed a million pots and pans. Not that we had that many but that I washed what we had a million times. Right in the middle of everything Mama made Papa stop and unpack the dining table from Kansas that Gran'pa Murdock made out of walnut. I used our last bit of beeswax shining it up and there wasn't

any earthly sense in it because Mama covered the shine
with a long tablecloth pieced out with a sheet. Of
course we couldn't get the table into the soddy, so it
was set up under the cottonwood.

"You sure put the big pot in the little one and made
the skillet into hash!" Papa grumbled at the to-do. "I
don't see why you women can't do things without such
a fuss. Just put out vittles a-plenty an' let 'em all sit
down and fall to."

Mama stood there with her hands on her hips and
her eyebrows up, looking at him till he quit talking. He
was put out because he had to stand up to eat breakfast; there wasn't a bit of space left to sit down. Every-
place was covered with things for the dinner. It was
awful to eat mush and smell gingerbread! Mama
wouldn't let us touch a thing that was ready for the
dinner.

"It's the least we can do," she said over and over.
"We'd never in the world have got the house moved by
ourselves. Joe, did you remember to send word to
Brother Simmons to be sure and come?"

"He was out working on the house yesterday. I gave
him a special invitation."

"When we get the schoolhouse, maybe he'll come out
and preach."

"One thing at a time," Papa yelped, "one thing at
a time!"

It looked like all the county was there for the last day of the moving. Everybody that came brought something to eat. Mrs. Gurdy came early and Mrs. Ryman groaned when she saw her.

"I can't eat after that woman, Louise, I just can't!"

"Shhhh!" Mama said, "she means well."

"I aimed to bake up somethin'," Mrs. Gurdy said, "but I never got 'round to it. I brought a little mess o' roastin' ears I thought you might use. Garv'ry!" She bawled out his name like a bull calf and around the corner came Garvery lugging a washboiler of corn.

"That's real nice of you," Mama said, "and we sure thank you for all the help you've been to us moving the house. Look what nice corn, Amy."

Mrs. Ryman was as polite as a basket of chips and she and I shucked the corn together. "At least we can boil it," she whispered. I smiled but I didn't think it was very nice. Grownups sure do a lot of pretending and call it politeness. How are you supposed to know which is which?

There were some late tomatoes and some shucky beans and a dish of . . . ugh . . . okra—and some lye hominy. There were sand plum pies and vinegar pies and Tyler Evans brought two cans of peaches from Merton's Store. Mr. and Mrs. Merton brought the preacher with them and a dish of scalloped cove oysters! I didn't get any because I knew Mama would give

me hail Columbia if I took something there wasn't
enough of to go around. When I get rich I'm going to
have oysters every day. Tom had shot some prairie
chickens and Mama baked them up with dressing, and
she killed the old hen that hadn't laid an egg since she
came down from Kansas and boiled her and made
dumplings. The meat was tough but the dumplings
and gravy were larruping! The most important thing
was the ham. Gran'pa Murdock sent it and it was cured
by his own secret receipt; it came by way of some folks
traveling to Texas and Papa asked them to stay to the
dinner but they had to go on and a good thing—I never
did get all their children counted up! Mama boiled it
on Friday and it made my stomach growl just to smell
that ham smell!

Brunner's brought smearcase cheese and sliced
onions in vinegar. Espeys brought light rolls that
weren't very light. They brought a pound of hard
candy, too, and Warren gave me a piece he'd sneaked
out. It was only polite for me to take it, and besides I
was starving.

It was before noon that the teams brought the Diamond to the spot Mama had picked. There were so
many to help that the work went fast. The men pulled
and hauled and yelled at each other and the teams till
it was hard to tell what was going on. All the women
and girls and little kids were supposed to stay back by

the soddy but they kept getting in the way. Mama was running around trying to get the dinner fixed and trying to get Papa to tell her when they'd be ready to eat and trying to keep the little kids shooed away from the table. The dust was terrible and the flies were worse and I was supposed to stand and fan the food but I saw it happen. I saw the Diamond come off the jacks and shudder and settle and be quiet. We had a house!

The folks were all yelling and clapping and I was glad, honest I was. But I had a funny knot in my stomach and something flew into my eye and I dropped the pleated paper I was fanning with and ran around behind the soddy and leaned up against it.

When I opened my eyes there was Mr. Runninghorse standing there. He smiled at me and I had a feeling that he knew how I felt about the Diamond and the soddy.

"That old Diamond—be good house," he said and I nodded. The ache was going out of my stomach. "That hard word?" he said, "That Con—Con—?"

I laughed because all of a sudden I knew he knew how I felt and words didn't make any difference.

"We're sure glad you came, Mr. Runninghorse." I said it just the way I'd heard Mama saying it all morning. "And we thank you for all you've done to help us get moved."

We were both smiling when we went around the corner of the soddy.

Folks were milling around and kids were already climbing on the blocks the Diamond was propped up on. I saw Mama pull Papa's arm and he shook his head but she grabbed him again and he finally nodded and climbed up on Espeys' spring wagon.

"Yea, Joe!" Mr. Gurdy yelled and Mrs. Gurdy grabbed *his* arm!

"Well, folks," Papa said, "I'm not much for speech makin'. Usually leave the talkin' to the womenfolks in my family—" that started the men to laugh— "But I just want to say 'thanky' for all the work you've done, helpin' us to get started and I want you to know you've

got call on my time from now on. There's not a better set o' neighbors, not from here to Kansas!"

They all clapped again and Mr. Gurdy kept yelling "Speech!" till Mrs. Gurdy hauled him out of sight. "Now folks, I think that's about enough talk. We want you all to stay to dinner and take potluck with us. If we can stand it every day, you can stand it for one meal."

He climbed down and Mama shook her head like she was pleased and put out at the same time.

Then all the neighbors gathered 'round and Brother Simmons asked the blessing and we began to eat.

After dinner when nobody was in a hurry to get back to work Mama commenced to look for Tom to get him to draw water for dishwashing. I knew where he was, back of the Diamond with the other boys telling them the tales Mr. Runninghorse had told us about Skip Rentner and the bullethole in the wall. He had them all lined up to put a finger into the bullethole and he was charging so much a poke. When Mama found out she almost went straight up.

First off she made Tom give back everything he'd collected. A jackknife with one blade gone, some snelled fishhooks, a box of California Fruit Gum, a bottle of bait for traps that smelled horrible, even through the cork—that was from Garvery—and I don't know what-all else. She gave Tom a talking-to about folks that make money off their neighbors.

Tom stood with his face like a sliced tomato, and the boys were kind of hangdog looking, too. Mama made them all come over to the bullethole.

"Now boys, you know what this is, you've seen it and touched it, and it's not a thing in the world but a nick in a piece of wood. It's nothing to be proud of, like, say, a stand of wheat or a field of corn or a good team you've raised from colts, or a store you've built up. There's not a single one of you that couldn't do a better day's work this minute than either one of the rapscallions that were mixed up in this—and them grown men. Now I've decided to leave that bullethole right where it is so all of you can come see it if you get any fancy ideas about outlaws—just a chunk of nothing—just a hole in the wall!" Then Mama smiled and when she smiles after she's mad it's kind of wonderful. "And no charge!"

The boys melted away without saying much, and Tom was so hacked he went to the well and drew three tubs of water without stopping. But Mama was still upset.

"I've just got to stop folks from thinking about this as the Diamond," she said to Mrs. Ryman over the dishpan. "I don't care what Joe says, it's bad for Tom."

"Oh he'll forget it. It's just his age."

"It's like the place was—haunted," Mama said. She went on washing dishes, then all at once she took her hands out of the water, dried them on her apron, took off her apron and handed it me. "Hang this up, Betsy, and come along with me, all of you. I've got an idea."

That's how it came about that we had a dedication service over our house. Just the same was we had over our church back in Kansas when the Presiding Elder took dinner at our house and ate four wishbones. (Gran'ma Murdock said I ought to be ashamed for counting, but Gran'pa said it was no more'n the man deserved.)

Jenny and Jeanie played "Bringing in the Sheaves"

on their mandolins and Mrs. Ryman led singing. Nell read a poem she'd written, "Our New Home in Oklahoma Territory." It wasn't as bad as it might have been. I mean it wasn't all fancied up; except she did put in, "the rising of the nightly gale, carries the coyotes' musical wail." And it you've ever heard coyotes—they're not musical.

Mama opened her Bible then and I thought she was going to read the scripture but instead she handed it to me and pointed to the 127th Psalm. If she'd told me ahead I'd have been too scared but that way I just opened my mouth and read, "Except the Lord build the house, they labour in vain that build it. . . ." It did seem like David, way back there, had known about us and our house.

Then Brother Simmons talked. He said that the old Diamond had given shelter to the homeless and food to the hungry for years, not asking who came within its walls. Now things had changed and it wasn't a public house any more but the home of a family and he hoped we'd all think of it that way. He said most of us had come to the Strip to get a new start in life so we ought to be willing to let a house have the same chance. Then he asked a blessing on the new life in the old walls and on everybody who had helped. It wasn't very long that he talked but when he got through I felt like we really had a home.

"Now men, get those hammers goin'," he finished, "so's you can get in town to preachin' tomorrow."

But that wasn't all. Not by a long shot! Mama stepped right up there beside him, just like she was a preacher herself and called out, "Folks, as long as we're gathered together, everybody that thinks we ought to have a school meet over in the shade back of the soddy."

Papa's face was downright funny!

"No rest for the wicked," he said, but I had a sneaking feeling he was proud of Mama.

That night after the neighbors had gone and the dust had settled our family walked around the house. We didn't talk much. There'd been a lot of talking that day and it was nice to be quiet. Peaceful.

"We've come a long way," Mama said after awhile. She looked northeast toward where we'd come onto the claim after the Run.

"A long way," Papa said. He looked out at the corral where Puss and Bess were and I knew he was thinking about how they'd brought us here and that Mr. Grubb had sent word he'd be around for them on Monday. "But it's worth it."

The new house looked big and empty and kind of lonesome standing there by itself. It seemed a shame for it to be dragged across the prairie and nobody even sleep in it in the first night.

"I want to sleep in the new house." I said, "Pretty please, Mama."

"Why Betsy . . . by yourself . . . with no furniture. . . ."

"Oh let her do it," Papa said, "she can make down a pallet."

"Please, Mama, I'm not afraid."

"She won't be more'n a stone's throw from us," Papa said.

"I think it's crazy," Mama said, "but I'm too tired to argue. Go ahead."

It was fun dragging quilts in and making a pallet and having a whole big house all to myself, except for Rex. I was so tired I went right to sleep.

I don't know how long I'd slept when I waked up. Wide awake as a hoot owl! There was starlight outside and the shadows inside looked blacker than anything I'd ever imagined. The crossbars over the windows to hold the frames while the house was being moved made big X marks. All the scary things I hadn't thought of since I was little began to creep around in my head. A coyote yapped and another answered, closer and closer. Coyotes are cowards, anybody can run 'em off flapping a dishrag but at night they sound like wolves. Hundreds of wolves. Something skittered across the darkest corner of the room. A mouse? Or maybe. . . .

"It's like the place was—haunted." I could hear

Mama saying that. My knees crept up to my chin and I wanted to pull the quilt over my head but I didn't dare to move. The back of my neck was solid ice. I tried to remember what Brother Simmons said and what I'd read in the Psalms but all I could do was listen to the creak and groan of timbers, and think about Blacky Adams, shot right over there, and Skip Rentner's mark on the wall.

"If Skip comes back it'll be to the Diamond," Mr. Runninghorse's voice whispered. And outside I heard a horse, singlefooting across the prairie. My teeth chattered and I couldn't stop them. Skip Rentner was coming back!

Why had I stayed? Why wasn't I in my safe bunk bed, curled around Nell's back? "Not more'n a stone's throw . . ." Papa had said.

"Papa!" I croaked. "Papa!" but I could hardly hear myself.

Then I remembered Rex. He was right at my feet, as sound asleep as one of those cast iron dogs that rich folks put on their lawns. I moved my leg down and shoved him. In stories the faithful dog always warns the family of danger. Rex just yawned and stretched and moved closer on my pallet.

"You Rex!" I jumped up and grabbed him by the scruff of his neck. The hoof beats were coming closer and closer. I hauled Rex to the door and shoved him out. "Sick 'em—sick 'em!" Out he ran, wagging his tail!

In the dim starlight I could see the black shape of the rider and the horse. If Skip Rentner shot Rex—I ran out into the night calling for Rex and my white nightgown spooked the horse and he went rearing and bucking all over the yard. I caught Rex and we huddled up against the Diamond waiting for a chance to make a dash to the soddy. Then the rider got the horse quiet and sidled over to us.

"Betsy Boy? What're you doin', hoot-owlin' around?"

It was Tyler Evans! I was so mad I could have bit nails in two.

When my mad simmered down I felt kind of relieved. Suppose it *had* been Skip Rentner? Of course I didn't let on to Tyler what I'd been thinking. I asked him whatever in the world was he doing riding around the country in the dead of night?

"Couldn't get to sleep. I guess a feller that's been batchin' isn't up to the fancy kind of food I took on here at the house-raisin'. I rec'lected that I forgot to leave a letter for Miss Louise that I picked up in Hardpan so I took a notion to ride over and leave it in the door of your new house." He got off his horse and handed me a thick crackly envelope. I sniffed. Perfume!

"Who do you reckon it's from?"

Tyler took out a match and scratched it along the leg of his jeans. The little yellow flame wavered in the wind. He held it cupped in his hands and we put our heads together and read the return address in fancy curly writing. "Miss Charity Whipple. Jourdan Bend, Kansas, Care of Mrs. Egbert Whipple."

"It's the one Mama asked to come and be our teacher."

"I've got a feeling she's comin'," Tyler said, kind of solemn for him. "I've got a real strong feeling."

The match burned down to a curved-down black stick. He flipped it away but the yellow flame stayed inside my eyes for a minute. I could smell the perfume from the letter and hear the night wind singing past my ears. *She was coming.* I knew it, too!

"Get back to your pallet, Betsy Boy. I'm not sleepy yet awhile. I'll stand night guard out here for a little."

All of a sudden I was sleepy. I snuggled down in my quilts and Rex snuggled down on my feet. I could see the tiny red of Tyler's cigarette and I felt snug as a bug in a rug.

The last thing before I went to sleep I thought about Miss Charity. I was sure she was coming, but what would she be like, and would she want to stay in the Strip? She just *had* to stay! Stay with us in our new house and teach at the school that was so new it wasn't even there yet.

Chapter 5

It didn't take us long to get into the new house. Papa fixed the floors and the roof and put our two glass windows from the soddy in. Then we just moved all our stuff in and scattered it around and unpacked the things from Kansas. We kind of rattled around with an upstairs and a downstairs after living in one room and we didn't have enough furniture but, shoot! We were happy as June bugs!

Almost every day Mama would say to Papa, "Oh Joe, I'm so thankful for this house!"

Once he said, "I declare, Louise, I guess I didn't realize what you went through. I should never have brought you down here to live in a soddy."

"The very idea!" Mama put her arms around him right in front of all of us. "I'd never have let you come without me. And I'm glad we lived in a soddy. Glad! You have to live in a soddy to appreciate a house."

It wasn't any time at all after Mama called the meeting at our house-raising till the neighbors got together and put up a sod schoolhouse. On Gurdys' corner!

Mama was flabbergasted. She had a spot on our claim picked to donate. Mrs. Ryman said with two sets of twins to get schooling she thought it was up to *them*. Espeys told Papa they thought of offering but held back on account of Mama's feelings, she being the one to bring it up and all.

Well, Mr. Gurdy offered first and that was that. Not to take his offer would have made bad feeling. When the work of building the school began nobody saw hide nor hair of him. Then he had the gall to turn up on the last day of work and want to have the school named Gurdyville! Papa said why not name it Skiprock School since they'd used sod instead of rock to build it. They had a show of hands and Papa's name won. In fact, there was only one vote for Gurdyville.

Tyler and I had been right about Miss Charity's letter. It did say she would come and teach if they would accept somebody without experience or a Normal certificate. All she had to offer was that she liked children and she'd been through high school and had one year at a young ladies' seminary and her best subjects there were English and Hand-Painted China.

Mama showed the letter to the school committee. There was some grumbling about the hand-painted

china. Mr. Espey said he hoped she didn't figger on
teaching nothing like that. It was bad enough to have
to eat off tin plates without having 'em gaumed up with
flowers and doo-dads. In the end I think it was the perfume in the letter that brought 'em around. I saw Mr.
Ryman sniff it twice. Anyway, it was decided to ask
Miss Charity to come and the salary was thirty dollars
a month, with every pupil to pay one dollar a month
and no cut rate for big families.

We didn't have to pay because Miss Charity was to
stay at our house. Her room was to be upstairs, across
from Nell's and mine. We put the rose and ring quilt
on the bed there, and the oak dresser with the big mirror in the corner, and the braided rug Gran'ma Murdock sent on the floor. It was fit for a queen.

Nell wrote a poem and stuck it in the mirror:
"Thrice Welcome, Fair Teacher." (Only she had to
make it Teacher Fair because hardly anything rhymes
with 'teacher' except 'preacher.') Mama made us brush
up on our spelling and arithmetic. She fixed up our
clothes and Nell had a new dress and I had one of
Nell's that she had hardly worn and it didn't matter
because Miss Charity had never seen it anyway. I guess
Mama told us a million times not to expect favors because we were "connected" with the teacher and to say
Miss Charity, no matter if we were kinfolks. Kissing
kin, anyway. Papa whittled wooden pegs and fixed them

in the wall to hang clothes on. She was to arrive at Vigil—the nearest railroad station—August 25. Everybody was happy and excited about Miss Charity but Tom.

Tom was really soured on school. He and Garvery had scared up some traps and were figgering on spending the winter trapping.

"Trapping what?" Papa said. Tom sulked for three days.

I could tell that Papa felt bad about Tom and he did all sorts of little things to try to make friends again. But Tom's just like Papa—stubborn as a bogged-down mule. Finally Papa said that Tom could take the day before we went to meet Miss Charity and go hunting. Not even do chores. He took the gun down from over the door and the wooden box with shell cases and shot out from under the kitchen safe and said "Go to it, boy, an' good huntin'."

Tom brightened up at that. "I think I'll take Rex, too. He's no good for anything but rabbits but he'll be company."

Talking that way about Rex put my back up. "If Rex goes, I go, too."

"Aw, gee whizz!"

Papa frowned. He hates for us to fuss. "It's Betsy's dog and her say."

I wouldn't look at Mama. I knew she was waving

her eyebrows to try to make me act like a lady. I didn't want to act like a lady. "If Rex goes, I go too, and that's that!"

It's not much fun to go along when you're not wanted. Tom wouldn't even walk alongside of me. He stalked ahead, his back stiff as a board. Rex raised a few cottontails and some jackrabbits but Tom couldn't shoot for sour apples. He missed three shots in a row. I snickered.

"I'm goin' home," he said. "Rather do chores than hunt with you."

I was sorry and I said so. Tom wouldn't even answer. I wished I'd stayed home in the first place but how can you undo what you've done? It's like trying to unscramble eggs. I straggled along after Tom and Rex came back with me. I was walking with my hand on Rex's head when he stiffened and growled.

"Tom! Something's up ahead."

"Awrrrr," Tom growled. Just like Rex, he growled.

"There is, too! Rex won't move. Maybe it's a panther!"

"More likely a mud turtle if that mutt's noticin'." Just the same, he turned around and for the first time that morning he acted interested.

"Let's go on the scout," I said, and got down on the grass. That was the way we used to play outlaw and sheriff. We slithered along on our knees and elbows till we got to the top of a little rise in the prairie.

"For Pete's sake!" Tom started laughing, and so did I. Down in the little hollow below us was a family of skunks. A mama and three kits. In the sunshine their black and white fur looked as if it had just been cleaned up for comp'ny. They were the cutest things! They chased each other and jumped stiff-legged and piled onto their mama. One of them took out after a cabbage butterfly and the mama trotted after him and made him come right back. She cuffed him and he tumbled over and the others jumped in and they kept playing.

"Skunk hides bring a good price," Tom said.

"Oh Tom! Not those cute little things!"

"Girls!" Tom snorted. "Skunks are the worst chicken thieves in the country. I oughta shoot 'em right now, but their fur's not prime. Besides, I got 'nother idea." There he sat on the grass, hugging his knees and grinning. I begged and begged but he wouldn't tell me what he was laughing about. All he'd say was, "Boy, oh boy!"

"All right for you, Tom Richardson! I'm goin' home and tell Mama how mean and hateful you're actin'."

He let me get up and start down the rise toward our house. Then he came after me. "Betsy, if I tell you

will you cross your heart and hope to die that you
won't tell anybody?"

> *"Cross my heart and hope to die,*
> *If what I say is any lie."*

I got it all out in one breath. "Now, tell."

Tom put his thumbs in his belt and rocked on his
heels, the way Papa does. "Oh, I was just thinkin' about
these pore little skunks. Out here in the Strip, growin'
up without any schoolin'. . . . I figgered it was my
bounden duty to get 'em started in to school."

"Tom—you wouldn't!"

"I would so. I never asked to have any old school
started. Time they run four skunks out of a soddy
they'll think twic't about havin' school."

"How'll you get the skunks to go to the school?"

"That's simple," he bragged. "First off I'll get out
the rabbit gum that me'n Garvery made from that
dead limb off the cottonwood . . . ." A rabbit gum's
a piece of hollow log with one end closed up. The other
has a door that drops when the animal gets inside. "I'll
set it right down there. Now when those kits an' their
ma get in the trap, I'll have me a gunny sack ready to
throw over the end, see? Then I'll pull up the door,
pour 'em *into* the sack, pick up the sack on a stick—"

" 'Bout that time you'll get good and skunked yourself."

"Oh no! No skunk can spray you if his feet's off the ground. Didn't you know that?" Tom stopped to laugh. "Then I'll carry 'em over to the schoolhouse, prize open the window, pour 'em *out* of the sack—and skedaddle. The skunks'll know what to do from there on. Boy, oh boy!"

I'm ashamed to admit it, but I got to laughing along with Tom. The thought of those little skunks, all black and white, neat as pins, sitting on school benches, and their mama up at the teacher's desk. . . .

"Tom, what about Miss Charity?"

"Let 'er go back to Kansas and teach school there."

"Mama'll be mad. She'll be awful, awful, awful mad."

"Who's goin' to tell her? You crossed your heart."

"That's right. I did."

All afternoon my stomach hurt from wanting to tell Mama what was about to happen. She'd been working at the schoolhouse all morning with Mrs. Ryman, and now she was going over our house with a finetooth comb. But whenever I opened my mouth to say a word I'd remember about crossing my heart and my teeth would clamp together.

At supper Tom didn't miss a mouthful. He talked to Papa about hunting as if he had a special pass to the Happy Hunting Grounds. Nell kept worrying Mama about getting the hem in her new school dress. I sat and pushed beans around on my plate.

We had a spelling lesson after supper. Papa gave out
the words because Mama had her mouth full of pins
for putting the hem in Nell's dress. I'm the best speller
in our family, and that's not bragging, it's just the
plain truth, but I was so bothered that I missed words
I hadn't missed in years. And Tom, who can't spell
worth a whoop in a rain barrel, put me down three
times! That sure tickled Papa.

"You'll have to get up early in the morning to beat
Tom, Betsy."

I missed the next word he gave out but I didn't care.
All of a sudden I knew what to do. "Get up early in
the morning to beat Tom"—well, that was just what
I'd do. I'd sneak out to that trap myself and let the
skunks out!

All night I kept waking up for fear I'd oversleep.
When the black sky began to lighten around the edge
of the east I knew it was time. Tom was still asleep, and
so was everybody else in the house. I slipped down the
stairs, waiting between each creak, carrying my shoes
with me. Outside I sat on the step to put on my shoes.
It was a strange time—not real dark, and not yet
light. There were some scattered stars, and one real
bright one. I like the part in the Bible about the "morning stars sing together," I thought that if I could be
quiet enough I might hear them. Then I remembered

there wasn't time to sit and star-gaze. I had to hurry!

Rex came up and put his cold nose in my hand. I tiptoed till I got clear of the yard, then I started to run. My feet and my heart went bump-bump-bump bumpity-bump. Rex ran with me quiet as a shadow, and I guess that shows he's a smart dog! A lot smarter than Tom Richardson thinks.

I found the rise and I went right to where we'd been when we saw the skunk family. I'd brought a long stick to trip the rabbit gum. Rex grabbed at the stick and began to whine. I thought he wanted to play and I shushed him and got down in the grass and slithered along with the stick out in front. Rex got frantic. He barked and pawed at me. Then he caught the hem of my dress in his teeth and growled.

I turned around to make him let go, and there, coming right at me was the mama skunk! I don't know which of us was more surprised but I do know she was quicker! She planted her feet, lifted her black and white plume and . . . . Whew!

Rex ran, squalling and yelping. I scrambled up and

tried to run but I was blind and choking. Oh, there just aren't any words to tell what it's like!

I coughed and choked and threw up till the bottom of my stomach hit the top. My eyes were burning and watering. I didn't know whether it was better to breathe or choke to death. The mama skunk had disappeared in the grass. When I got so that I could see just a little I started for home. Every little bit I'd stop and get sick all over again.

I could hear the rumpus Rex was raising long before I got to our house. He was tearing round and around barking high and shrill. Mama and Papa and Nell and Tom were all standing out in the yard and Papa had the gun. Rex came charging around the house and stopped, pawing at his nose and ki-yi-ing, like he'd gone mad. Papa raised the gun but I yelled and he lowered it.

Mama ran for me, then, but when she got within nose-shot she stopped in her tracks.

"Betsy! Stay where you are! Don't come one step closer!"

Now I know what it's like to have nobody in the world love you.

There's no use in going over all the things Mama did to get me un-skunked. Just to think about them makes my skin hurt clear to the bone. Worse than that, even, was the way she and Papa plainly thought I was just roaming around the claim at that time of the morning without sense enough to keep out of the way of trouble. Or skunks! And Tom didn't say a word. Just scrubbed on poor old Rex, looking as if butter wouldn't melt in his mouth. *Just wait,* I kept saying inside, *just you wait!*

"I give up," Mama said when she'd washed my hair three times. "It'll just have to wear off."

"We got to get on the way to Vigil!" Papa shook his watch at Mama. "Forget about Betsy's hair."

"I can't, and neither can anybody else."

"I won't go," I said. "I won't go and meet Miss Charity smelling like a—like this!"

"You can't stay here by yourself," Mama said distracted. "It'll be dark before we get back."

"I—I'll stay home with her," Nell said. "Poor Betsy!"

"No," Mama said. "Two girls alone won't do. It'll have to be Tom."

"Me?" Tom yelped. "Why pick on me?"

"We got to get started," Papa said. "A green team an' a long trip." ·

"Now Tom," Mama said, "I'll bring you something nice from Vigil. Betsy, there's plenty in the house to eat. Nell bring me my hat, and take my apron in. And Betsy—uh, try to stay outside for awhile, at least. And wash your hair again with bluing; that might help. There's dried peach pie. . . . Yes, Joe, I'm comin' . . . and Betsy . . . ."

The mustang team we'd traded for to take the place of Puss and Bess wouldn't stand two minutes so Papa drove off with Mama still telling me things to do about my hair and what to put out for dinner and Tom still saying, "Geeeeeee Whizzzzz . . . *why me?*"

When our folks were just a cloud of dust and a rattle Tom and I turned around on each other.

"Makin' me stay home to look after you! Sufferin' snakes!"

"Tryin' to break up Skiprock School! And getting me skunked up!"

"Aw, how'd I know you'd go pokin' around? Besides, I wasn't really goin' to do it. I *wasn't*. I was just havin' fun talkin' about it. Cain't girls understand anything?"

"I wouldn't believe you on a stack of Bibles. When Mama gets home I'm goin' to tell her the whole thing. JUST YOU WAIT!"

"You crossed your heart," Tom looked scared. "You hoped to die. Dead."

"Well, I'm uncrossin' my heart. I 'figgered out how to do it while Mama was washing my head with ashwater." I made a cross sign backwards. "Now you listen to me—'Lie-any-is-say-I-what if-die-to-hope-and-heart-my-cross.' There!"

"Who cares? Go on an' tattle. I won't be here."

"And where will you be, pray tell?" I got that out of one of Nell's poems and I thought it sounded real uppity but Tom didn't pay me any mind. He walked off talking to himself out loud.

" 'Bring you something real nice from Vigil!' Awwr! Do they think I'm a baby? Stay home to look after a girl with no more sense than to get skunked. Make a little old joke and act like it was bloody murder! Awrrr! Well, I'm gettin' out. There's places I can go. And it ain't to school! Awrrrrr!"

The kitchen door slammed. Later it slammed again. I wouldn't look around. I just pretended to watch a scissortail across the road catching bugs in the air too small to see. If I could be a bird I'd like to be a scissortail. Or would it be better to be a mockingbird?

I washed my hair one more time and the bluing didn't do a thing except make it look like kind of dauncy. It still smelled, or I guess it did; my nose wasn't any account by this time. My back and neck were tired from bending over the wash bench. I sat down on the back step in the sun with a towel for a pillow. If I could have gone inside and taken a nap . . . but I didn't want to get Miss Charity's room all you-know-what. I was sleepy anyway from getting up before day, and with the sun, and the tiredness . . . my eyelids wouldn't stay up.

When I waked up I blinked at the shade of the cottonwood. It was slanting left. Why, it must be past noon! I stood up and there were needles and pins in my right foot; that meant I was going on a journey. I hopped around to get my foot awake, wondering where the journey would be, and all the time calling, "Tom . . . Tommmmmm . . . dinner . . . Tom. . . ."

Nobody answered. A queer little echo came from the house.

"Tommm . . . dinnertime . . . Tommm. . . .

A house tells you when there's nobody in it. I thought Tom might be around the soddy or back by the corral and I went down that way with my voice getting louder and louder till I was screeching.

"TOMMMM . . . TOM EEEEEE. . . .

I came back to the house and sat down on the step again. The needles and pins were out of my foot. Maybe I wasn't going on a journey. Or maybe the sign was meant for somebody else. I jumped up, scared. Then I remembered there'd be one thing sure. Tom wasn't likely to miss a meal, and if he'd eaten while I was asleep he'd never wash the dishes. I forgot all about what Mama said and ran inside. Everything was just the way Mama left it. I ran into every room in the house; I even looked under the beds.

There wasn't any place to look any more. I came down to the kitchen and tried to think what to do next.

My stomach growled and I realized I hadn't had anything to eat since last night on account of being too upset over the skunk to eat breakfast. I went over to the safe and opened the door. Propped up against a bowl of cold mush for frying was a note from Tom.

"To who it may consern. I have gone away to join an outlaw band. Donut try to find me. Love. Thos. Richardson." He'd scratched out the "love" but I could read it.

The first thing I thought was that Tom never could spell.

Then something hit me right in the middle. Tom was gone, really and truly gone. The journey sign had been for him. He'd meant what he said about leaving home. I sat, plunk, down in a chair by the safe. Tom had gone to join the outlaws.

What in the world was I going to tell Mama? And Papa that thought Tom was the finest boy that came down the pike? And Nell with all her talk about Honor and Holy Grails—not but what some of those knights don't sound kind of outlawish to me. And Miss Charity? What would she think? Maybe she'd go right back to Kansas. And part of this was my fault for being hateful about letting him take Rex hunting.

I thought about Tom the way I hadn't for a long time. The way he'd climb the highest walnut trees back in Kansas and thrash down nuts for me. How he'd let me beat at checkers sometimes . . . it was the only way I ever got to beat. How he pushed Fatty Orten in the face for grabbing my licorice whip. And he let me read his Nick Carter books that Mama didn't know he had. If only he'd come back! I wouldn't tell Mama about the skunk. I crossed my uncrossed heart and said:

> *"Cross my heart and hope to die,*
> *If what I say is any lie."*

I couldn't go any further. I started bawling.

That was how it happened I didn't hear a horse come up till the man was standing at the door. A stringy man with his hat down low so I couldn't see his face. He leaned against the door like he was too tired to stand straight, or like his gun belt was too heavy for him.

"Howdy. Anybody to home?"

"Nobody but me," I hiccupped. "Tom's gone off. He's run away to be an outlaw and it's part my fault and I don't know what to tell Mama and—"

"You say there's nobody here but you?"

"They'll be back at dark."

The stranger shoved back his hat and I got a look at his face. He had a black stubble of beard and light blue eyes and he was dirty. That sounds rude to say of a stranger but this one looked as if he hadn't washed— or had a chance to wash—for anyway a week.

"Won't you come inside and sit down?" I opened the door.

The stranger shifted his gunbelt and stared into the room. Then I saw his nostrils flare out, like a skittish horse.

"I'm sorry," I said, "a skunk got me."

"I *mean!*" he said, and came in the house. "Got any cawfee?"

"I can make you some fresh in a minute . . ."

He took the coffee right out of my hands and lifted a lid on the stove and poured about half of it onto the coals. Real coffee that Mama had bought special for Miss Charity! The smoke came up in a thick cloud. The stranger took hold of my shoulders and held me down, right in the smoke. I coughed and choked but he held me like iron, turning me this way and that. When the smoke died off he let me come up for air.

"Got skunked plenty, back in Missouri, when I was a boy. This was my old ma's sure cure. You ain't so bad, now."

And sure enough, he was right. I was awful mad about being pushed around and thinking about Mama's expensive coffee, but I was sure glad to smell like a human being . . . or even a cup of coffee . . . instead of a you-know-what!

The stranger kept looking around our kitchen and frowning. He still had on his pushed-back hat, which is mighty poor manners. Something in me began to get uneasy. Manners aren't everything, but bad manners show which way the wind blows, Gran'ma Murdock says.

"Set me out some grub," he said, all at once.

"Why—why yessir," I said. I guess I should have asked him to eat before now but it was long past dinner time and with Tom gone I just forgot. I started to apologize.

"Cut out the gab and set it out. I got no time for talk."

I set out the things Mama had meant for Tom and me, and two plates. I was hungry but I couldn't seem to eat much for watching the stranger. I'd never seen anybody eat the way he did. As if he hadn't seen food since . . . well, since before he'd washed. But even while he was shoveling it in, on the point of his knife, he kept skinning his eye around our kitchen and staring through the open door into the parlor. He put the last bite of peach pie on his knife, gulped it down, wiped the back of his hand across his mouth, and got up and walked across the kitchen and into the parlor. He went straight to the bullet hole in the wall, fingered it, then he came back, stepping quiet as a cat.

"You folks lived here long?"

I was about to tell him how we'd bought the old Diamond, and moved it, and what Mr. Runninghorse said about the bullet hole, when I heard a horse singlefooting on the road outside.

"That's Tyler! He'll help me find Tom!" I ran for the door.

Before I was halfway there the stranger was in front of me and the look in his light blue eyes stopped me in my tracks.

"Set down an' finish yore meal." His voice was as hard and cold as his eyes. "No use gittin' the neighbors all stirred up."

"Yessir," I whispered. I couldn't swallow another bite. I pushed beans till the sounds of Tyler's horse's hoofbeats went clear away.

"Now do what you're told an' you won't git hurt," the stranger said. "Dump the rest of that grub in a poke and be quick about it. Got any money in the house?"

"In the china teapot," I said. Thank goodness Papa

had the rest of our money in his money belt. The stranger found three dollars and a half and two dimes. He sneered.

"Nesters! Ruin the country an' then go broke! Ain't wuth a man's time to clean out the county!"

I was mad enough to tell him a thing or two, but I was too scared to do it. I've thought of a thousand things since! He grabbed the sack of food out of my hands and slammed me into a kitchen chair.

"Set there!" He jerked down the tea towels drying over the stove and tied them together, then he tied my hands behind me to the chair.

"Please, mister," I said. "I've got to find Tom, my brother. I've got to."

"Shut up!" he jerked the knots tighter. "I'm leavin' an I don't want any blasted nester posse on my trail." That wasn't just what he said but I won't write down the real words, not even for my book. "Nothin'll happen to you if you keep quiet. When your folks git back I'll be outa the country."

"It's Tom. I've got to find Tom before he gets too far away."

"Run off, huh?"

"He's gone to join the outlaws. There's the note he wrote if you don't believe me."

The stranger squinted at the note. "I cain't read handwritin' so good."

"But it's true, and I've got to stop him. He wants to find Skip Rentner. He thinks—he thinks—" It was like the last piece of a jigsaw puzzle had dropped into place. I looked at the stranger. "Why, *you're* Skip Rent—" He smacked me across the mouth.

"Shut up!"

"You let my sister alone!"

It was Tom in the doorway with Papa's gun leveled at the stranger. His voice cracked but his eyes didn't waver.

The stranger's arms dropped to his sides. He smiled. It was the first time he'd smiled. His teeth were yellow but his smile warmed up his eyes. "Well, I'll be dog'. Pretty smart brother you got there, Sis. What outfit're you gonna join up with, Bud?"

"You turn her loose. You untie her."

"Why sure, it was just a kind of a joke. Just some-thin' she could tell the folks." He untied me and my hands hurt when the knots let go. "Now there, Sis." He turned back to Tom. "Be glad to speak to some o' the boys 'bout a sharp kid like you. Think you c'n shoot?"

"Sure I can," Tom said.

"I mean sure 'nough. Not just tote that old shot-gun of yore Pappy's around the claim."

"I c'n prove it," Tom said. "I c'n put a bullet in that knothole in the top rail of the fence."

"Bud, that's pretty fancy shootin'."

"Just watch me!" Tom turned around and aimed out the door.

"Don't, Tom!" I yelled but I wasn't near quick enough. Nobody could have been quick enough. The stranger was on Tom's back like a cat on a song sparrow. He twisted the gun out of Tom's hands, gave him a kick with his heavy boot and Tom was lying, doubled up on the floor, and I was backed up in the corner before I hardly knew what happened.

The stranger laughed but no sound came from back of his yellow teeth. "Mama's boy! You think any outfit'd take you on? Fallin' for the oldest trick in the business? Show off yore shootin'? I'll show you some real shootin'."

He looked around the room and everything he looked at was something I loved. Then he stepped backwards into the parlor and came out carrying Miss Sophy Sophronia, Nell's china-headed doll. Nell was too big to play with dolls but she wouldn't give up Miss Sophy Sophronia and always kept her dressed up, sitting on the cow-horn footstool.

"Please don't," I said. "She came from Kansas."

"Jayhawker, huh? I hate 'em."

He threw Miss Sophy Sophronia into the air, her petticoats flying; then there was that movement like lightning that Mr. Runninghorse told about. The gun blazed and the room was full of smoke and shaking with noise. Miss Sophy Sophronia's headless body fell in a heap. She was only a doll, only a stuffed, china-headed doll but I felt terrible, as if she were a real person, and I knew all of a sudden that he'd shot people, too, just the same way. It never had seemed true before, about Blacky Adams, but now it did.

"Now you two," he said, "I've messed around long enough. Get on yore feet and march."

Tom got up. I could tell it hurt him but he didn't complain. The stranger marched us down to the soddy and made us go inside. He told us we'd better not try to get out till dark or he'd come back and give us what he gave the play-dolly. Then he jerked the latchstring and tied it on the outside. We heard him ride off.

It was dark in the soddy. Papa had taken the glass windows for the new house and put wooden shutters on to keep out the rain.

"Are you hurt bad, Tom?"

"I'll live," Tom grunted, "but I sure wish I hadn't let that jessy get the jump on me. I was sure a gump!"

"You were not! You were brave and wonderful! The way you came back to protect me and stood up to him and all. Why . . ."

"Don't make me out no hero," Tom said. "I just—well, I got kind of hungry an' I thought about that dried peach pie an' I figured I might stick it out at home a while longer."

"I don't care what you say, you're a hero. Do you know who that was?"

"I kind of figgered," Tom said.

"It was Skip Rentner, that's who! He went right straight to that bullet hole in the parlor. Now—now I reckon you can't ever join his outfit."

"Me? Join up with him?" Tom said, as if he never had such an idea in his life. "Say, do you reelize he can't even read?"

"But he can shoot. Just like Mr. Runninghorse said. Like lightning."

"Awrrr, anybody can shoot with a little practice. But I hate it he got Papa's gun."

"Papa won't care, not when I tell him how brave you were."

"Brave? Me? I was scared spitless!"

"Golly gee whiz! So was I," I said.

"You didn't act scared." Tom reached over in the dark and tousled my hair. "For a girl, just a plain old girl, you did real good." After a minute he said, "Say, you don't—uh—smell any more."

"No. He did that anyway. He un-skunked me." I told Tom about the coffee on the coals, and all.

"Wait'll I tell 'em that at school!" Tom said. "Just wait till I give 'em the word at Skiprock School that Skip Rentner un-skunked my sister! Boy, oh boy!"

I didn't tell him I didn't want the school to know I

got skunked in the first place. If Tom was going to get any fun out of school I wanted him to go ahead. I was thankful we had our skins whole. Whenever I even thought about Skip Rentner and those pale blue eyes I got chills up my back. We'd come out of it lucky, except for Miss Sophy Sophronia.

"Hey, why don't we start tryin' to get out?" Tom said. "What're we settin' around here for?"

"I guess because he told us to. I wouldn't want to do anything against what he said."

"Awr," Tom growled, "he's miles away by now. Anyway, I'm not gonna have him tellin' me what to do."

He got up and started fumbling with the door, working it back and forth and easing the latchstring. After a little I helped him. If Tom wasn't going to be afraid of Skip Rentner, then I wasn't either. We worked and worked.

"I'm glad you're not going off to be an outlaw," I said, wiping the sweat off my face. It was awful hot in the soddy without any air much.

"I never really meant to," Tom said. "I mean, when I do, I'm gonna join a high class outfit. Not one that goes around pickin' on kids. Anyway, I got a lot of things to do first."

I guess it took an hour before we worked the latchstring through and got outside. That breeze sure felt good! We went to the house and sat on the steps. Every

now and then Tom'd nudge me with his elbow and
snicker.

"Coffee cup! That's what I'm gonna call you. Coffee
cup. You sure do smell like one."

I didn't care. Let him carry on. All I was was *thankful!*

It was sunset with the sky all pink and gold over blue
when our folks got home. We ran down the road when
we heard them coming and jumped in the wagon, telling about what happened. Mama turned white as a
sheet.

"The Lord watches over fools and children," she
said, "and both of 'em live on this claim. I'll never
leave you alone again, not as long as I live."

The wagon was jiggling but she hugged me and she
tried to hug Tom but he kept saying, "Awr," and moving away. Over Mama's shoulder I saw a young lady in
a blue linen coatsuit and a white shirtwaist sitting on
the folded-up quilts by Nell. She had the nicest smile I
ever saw in my life and when Mama introduced me she
said, "I've been wanting to meet you a long time, Betsy.
I'm going to need help at the school and I know I can
depend on you."

I wish Skip Rentner had come back right then! I
could have tied him in a double bow-knot!

Chapter 6

*A*fter all my talking and going-on Miss Charity was really in the Strip! Really on our claim, and really up in her room across from Nell's and mine. Sometimes things you think about a lot don't turn out so good. But Miss Charity did. She looked good enough to eat with her pretty clothes and her blue eyes and curly blonde hair, but just being pretty wasn't half of it. It was the *way* she was.

It's really hard to write down for my book what she was like. Telling about her clothes and her hair and her eyes is the same as saying that our homestead claim is west and south of Hardpan, O.T., and leaving it at that. It doesn't tell about the big cottonwood tree, or the wheat land that Papa and Tom were readying for a crop, or the hollow where we found the skunks, or the wind that made dust devils dance across the field. I know, now, how hard it is to find the way to say what a person looks like and I never have found the right words for Miss Charity.

She makes you feel good and happy inside. But don't you ever forget that she can get mad, too, and snatch you bald-headed if you don't mind in time of school. Most of the time she smiles, but I've seen her cry. Once she cried when she was reading out loud to the school, "Breathes there a man with soul so dead who never to himself hath said, this is my own, my native land. . . ." Then she wiped her eyes on a handkerchief with a pink tatted edge and said that the poem was really written about Scotland, but it's the way people everywhere feel about their homes, and we ought to feel that way about the Strip.

The first day of school she asked everybody's name and where they were from and to please stand and tell the thing they liked best about the Strip.

One of the littlest kids liked tumble-bugs the best!

Fatty Orten said he'd plunk for wild plum preserves. Warren Espey spoke up for Indian ponies. That stuck-up Elmyra Stoner said she didn't like anything *a-tall*. Can you imagine? Miss Charity said we'd all have to work at helping her find something to like but you can bet your bottom dollar *I* won't. Jenny and Jeanie liked the singings the neighbors had Sunday afternoons. Nell liked the Literaries, and no wonder, somebody always asks her to recite her newest poem. Tom and the Ryman twins—boy twins—spoke for hunting. When it came my time I said I liked Skiprock School. I really wanted to say Miss Charity but I was afraid she might think that was uppity, us being kind of kinfolks, and all.

Then came recess. Thad Ryman had a yarn ball so we played Ante Over across the schoolhouse. Miss Charity played and she could run as fast as any of the girls and catch as good as any of the boys. With all the running and catching her hair got ruffled up and her face pink. Then who should come rolling up in a buggy but Tyler Evans?

A buggy, mind you! I'd never seen Tyler anyway but on horseback, unless he was sitting at the table to eat. And here he was, large as life and twice as natural, driving a buggy. I ran out to ask him, how come?

He put me off slick as a whistle! Said he'd just taken the buggy off'n a fellow's hands to oblige him. Then

he told me he'd come to enroll in the school and please
take him to the teacher. That sounded mighty thin to
me, but I'd as soon kick a hog barefoot as argue with
Tyler so I took him into the schoolhouse. He was so tall
he had to bend down to get in at the door. Miss Charity
was at her desk—table, really—trying to get her hair
smoothed down.

"Miss Charity Whipple, I'd like you to make the
acquaintance of Mr. Tyler Evans that lives next claim
to ours," I said and I was proud that I sounded like
Gran'ma Murdock at church.

"I'm pleased to meet you," Miss Charity said. "Any
patron of our school is welcome to visit us at any time.
Which of these dear children belongs to you?"

Tyler got red in the face. So red his freckles just disappeared. He hemmed and he hawed; he backed and
he filled. He finally got it out that he didn't have any
children in Skiprock School. Didn't have any children
a-tall. Wasn't even married. Was just passing by, you
might say, and stopped in and. . . .

That was where he stuck and Miss Charity let him
stay stuck. She handed me the brass hand bell that Cousin Merthula had used when she taught school in
Nebraska and told me to get the school in from recess.
Mr. Evans, she said, was welcome to take a chair and
hear lessons.

There wasn't any chair, and we didn't have any lessons ready but Tyler didn't know that. He grabbed me by my left braid.

"Hold on a spell, Betsy Boy."

Miss Charity's eyebrows went up, just the way Mama's do. "Mr. Evans," she said in a voice like lemonade with ice and no sugar, "our school work must be carried on."

Tyler dropped my braid like it had turned to a red-hot poker. "I ask your pardon, ma'am. I'm strong for schoolin'. Fact is, I'm so strong for it that I figgered I oughta do somethin' special for the school. I mean havin' no kids of my own, not even married—"

"I believe you mentioned that," Miss Charity said.

"I've got more time on my hands than most menfolks with families—" Tyler stuck again and by this time the whole school was gathered around the door, sneaking peeks and snickering.

"Yes?" Miss Charity said in the same sweet-sour way.

"So I lit in an' made you-all a blackboard." Tyler got it all out in one breath.

"Why, that's very public-spirited of you," Miss Charity sweetened up a little. "I'm sure the children will be delighted."

Tyler went out to his buggy and brought in the blackboard. It was three wide boards nailed together, planed smooth, and painted with linseed oil and lamp black. He even had some chalk. (I found out later it came from a pool hall in Red Road.) He put the board up on the wall and Miss Charity smiled at him and stepped up and wrote, "Thank you, Mr. Tyler Evans,"

Thank you, Mr. Tyler Evans

with curlycues and a dove flying over the words. Then she asked him if he wouldn't like to say a few words to the school. But that was too much. Tyler skedaddled!

The rest of the first day we spelled and ciphered. Even Tom had a good time, though he'd have died before he'd say so.

School started slick as a greased pig going under a fence.

Books were all different. We brought what we'd been using back where we came from, or what our folks had. But we made out. We passed books around and doubled up. Sometimes four of us would squeeze together on a bench made for two. That is, until Elmyra Stoner's mother made her wear an asafetida bag to keep off colds. After that, nobody would sit with her.

Fatty Orten's father dug a well so that we wouldn't have to fill the water bucket at the creek. Mrs. Ryman made a gourd dipper. The ones that got the best marks got to pass the water bucket around during the morning and the afternoon. Miss Charity was awful finicky about taking a big drink and pouring what was left back in the bucket. If you let kids do that you didn't get to pass the bucket no matter how high your marks were. Mostly, I didn't get to pass the water bucket because of Deportment. That was my weakest subject. But I was strong in spelling.

Mama says I've no right to be stuck up about my spelling. It's a talent that I inherited from Gran'pa Murdock who was the best speller in Cloud, Indiana. A talent is something to be thankful for but not to brag about. I know that's true, but I couldn't keep from being proud of the medal.

The medal was Miss Charity's idea. She cut a star out of cardboard and covered it with silver paper. Garvery furnished the silver paper because it came around Mr. Gurdy's chewing tobacco. (It smelled a little tobacco-ery, too, for as long as we had it.) Whoever won the spelling match on Friday got to wear the medal till the next Friday, pinned on with a safety pin. The boys wouldn't wear it; they carried it in their pockets. The girls loved it. And I won the medal three weeks straight! Wouldn't you be proud?

Anyway, I got so that I felt like it was my very own property. Mama shook her head. She said I was due for a comeuppance. She read out of Proverbs, and looked straight at me, "Pride goeth before a fall and a haughty spirit before destruction."

I didn't mean to be proud or haughty; I just liked to win.

On Wednesday of the third week that I had the medal, Nell told me that Jenny told her that Milly Thompson told her that Elmyra Stoner said she was going to get that medal away from me if it killed her. I said pooh, and double pooh!

Elmyra Stoner was the only thing about Skiprock School that I didn't like. All the rest of us sat on back-less benches with our books on the dirt floor, but *her* mother brought a special desk to school, with a back and a place for books and said it was just for Elmyra because she was delicate. Delicate, my foot!

The day Fatty Orten tied her apron string to her fancy desk so that she couldn't stand up to recite she chased him half a mile and nearly beat the whey out of him when she caught him. She never swapped lunch and she had the fixiest lunch of anybody. But, shoot, I wasn't worried. I could outspell Elmyra and not use half the alphabet.

Mama said I'd better get to work.

Miss Charity offered to give out words to me.

Nell said I could use her dictionary, the one with the rhymes.

Well, I meant to do all those things. Honestly, I did. I just didn't get around to them. Wednesday night Tyler came over—seems to me he spent so much time on *our* claim he might as well prove up on it!—and Miss Charity popped a dishpan of popcorn, so I didn't get anything done. Thursday I meant to study hard at school but Mr. Thompson brought out the new stove.

You see, when our schoolhouse was built everybody gave what they could to furnish it but nobody had a stove to spare. Now that it was getting on to cool weather we had a Magic Lantern Show and raised $3.72 and $2.13 extra from the Cakewalk. Brother Simmons said a cakewalk was too near dancing for his taste but Mrs. Ryman said she didn't see any harm in it and it was an easy way to make money. Mr. Merton sold the committee the stove at almost cost price and threw in some coal, "So the pretty schoolmarm won't have to gather cow chips." (Mrs. Merton didn't like that one little bit!) Mr. Thompson hauled it out, as his part, but he said he couldn't set it up with all the school gawking at him so would Miss Charity please declare a half holiday. That was fine with us and we went to the creek and put our lunches together and had a picnic and skipped rocks and Miss Charity read to us from a new book she had, *The Hoosier Schoolmaster,* by Edward Eggleston, and it was a lot about a spelling match. Those funny people! The way they went on! But I can't see how I could have done any studying *that* day.

Thursday night Papa brought out from town the

late birthday present that came from Gran'ma Murdock. Gran'ma has twelve grandchildren and she never quite gets caught up on birthdays. That makes it more fun because any time in the year you're likely to get a birthday present. This time it was a book, *Swiss Family Robinson*. It had all kinds of pictures in it and I could hardly wait to get started reading it. Tom said it was really a boy's book and she probably meant it for him but I showed him, handwritten, right in the front, "To my dear grandaughter, Betsy, may she go as far in life as this family did in this story. Exselsior!"

Nell looked over my shoulder. "That means 'Onward, upward, ever.' It's in a poem by Henry Wadsworth Longfellow. It begins, 'The shades of night were falling fast. . . .'"

"I know how it begins and how it ends," I said. That sounds hateful, but once you let Nell get started saying poetry you're stuck for an hour.

"I know how *you're* going to end if you don't get out your speller."

"Go on upstairs and study," Mama put in. "I mean it!"

I took *Swiss Family Robinson* upstairs and put it on my bed. If I couldn't read it, I wasn't going to let anybody else! I opened it once again, just to see what Gran'ma had written. " . . . Exselsior!" I wondered if Mama had written to her about my spelling medal.

Then I thought I'd just glance at the first line. You know. And the first picture. The picture was a boy throwing a lasso around the neck of an ostrich! The line was "For many days we had been tempest-tossed. Six times the darkness closed over a wild and terrific scene. . . ."

When Nell came to bed and blew out the lamp I had just come to the place where a giant land crab takes in after Fritz. In the dark it all appeared before my eyes. I tried to tell Nell about it but she went to sleep.

I got up early the next morning and read some more while I was dressing . . . got my shoes on the wrong feet . . . and I took the book to school with me and held my geography in front of it. It didn't seem like any time at all till Miss Charity rapped with her pointer.

"Turn, rise, pass. Time for our weekly spelling match."

The way we did, the person that had the medal . . . me . . . I . . . Betsy Richardson . . . spelled against the whole school. The boys went down first; they always did. Then Jenny and Gert Jones and El-myra were left against me. Jenny and Gert both went down on "eclectic," that's a tricky word. So it was El-myra and me . . . I . . . Betsy Richardson.

Words popped back and forth, the way grains of corn pop in a hot skillet. From the way Elmyra started to spell before Miss Charity finished pronouncing, it was plain that she'd just about memorized the book. I began to feel shaky, especially in the bottom of my stomach where I always get scared first. Nell was smiling, proud as Punch. Tom wouldn't look at me, and that was a sign he was proud, too. Over in the corner Warren Espey wiggled his ears at Elmyra and went "heehaw" without making a sound. Even Miss Charity, I thought, smiled more at me than she did at Elmyra. They were all on my side and I couldn't let them down. I shut my eyes and spelled with all my might! That way, I can see the word in my mind's eye.

"Well!" Miss Charity shut the book. "You girls have finished the list. Let's call it a tie and you may share the medal this week."

"No!" the whole school yelled like a Comanche uprising. "No!"

Elmyra smiled like a pussycat. "I have a book that my mother used back in Ohio—if Betsy's not afraid."

I'd have jumped into a volcano before I'd have told that stuck-up Elmyra I was afraid of her or any of her kinfolks. But I was.

"It's fine with me," I said and everybody clapped and cheered.

Miss Charity looked worried. "Girls, the purpose of these spelling matches. . . ." Then she broke off. "All right. We'll go on." She took the dog-eared book Elmyra brought her. I knew what it was, the old blue-

backed speller. I'd seen it at Gran'pa Murdock's. Miss
Charity's forefinger traveled down a page. It was my
turn and I had a feeling she was looking for a word
she knew I could spell.

"Excelsior," she said, pronouncing every syllable.

I shut my eyes and I saw it plain on the front page
of *Swiss Family Robinson* in Gran'ma Murdock's cop-
perplate handwriting.

"E-X-S-E-L-S-I-O-R."

The schoolroom was too quiet. Somebody groaned.
Somebody snickered. I opened my eyes in time to see
Miss Charity shake her head.

"Next."

Elmyra smirked. Nell looked sick to her stomach. Tom leaned over to pick up something off the floor.

"E-x-C-e-l-s-i-o-r," Elmyra rattled off.

My nose stung and my eyes watered and I swallowed hard and started for my bench. All I wanted to do was get away from where everybody was staring at me.

"I'll thank you for that medal," Elmyra said.

Somehow I managed to get it off and hand it to her. My Gran'ma—my own Gran'ma Murdock that I loved next to my own family! Elmyra smirked as she put on the medal. She turned right around to Miss Charity.

"My mother says will you please and kindly come home to supper with us. It's going to be a celebration . . . about the medal."

"Why—thank you Elmyra, I don't know—" Then Miss Charity looked at me. "I think I will, Elmyra. Betsy, tell your mother I won't be home for supper."

"Yes ma'am," I said, though it just about choked me.

When school was dismissed I tried to get away as fast as I could but I didn't make it. Jenny and Jeanie and Mag Orten came around and said it wasn't fair, and Miss Charity shouldn't have used a book I hadn't studied. Warren Espey said how in the name of time did I miss an easy one like that when I could rattle off the hard ones? I made a snoot at him because I couldn't think of what to say and a person can't go around admitting her own grandmother doesn't know how to spell. Nell called after me, but I broke away and ran on, pretending not to hear. I just wanted to be by myself!

Off the road to our claim there's a little scrubby stand of blackjacks that grow near the ground and keep their leaves all winter. I made for that and squirmed in under the low branches. I could hear the rest of the school, hear them talking, and I knew they were talking about me. I felt sick and miserable and ashamed.

Miss Charity and Elmyra were the last to leave. I saw Elmyra prissing along, tossing her curls. Well, I may have just plain braids but her curls aren't *natural;* her mother puts them up in rags at night. Mama said *she* had better things to do than that. As for Miss Charity, I couldn't hardly look at her, it hurt me so bad. Celebrating that I lost a medal!

After a long time I crawled out and started for home, feeling as old and creaky as Aunty Persis who's ninety-seven this year. All of a sudden, there was Warren Espey, walking along beside me.

"I stayed to sweep up," he said, kind of mumbling.

It wasn't the truth; it was Thad Ryman's turn to sweep up. I just didn't feel like arguing. Warren dragged his feet and kicked up dust. It blew right into my face.

"Will you kindly stop that," I said, and right away I felt better. More like myself! We walked on a little ways.

"That old Elmyra makes me sick," he said.

"She can spell real good. Pretty good, I mean."

"Takin' Miss Charity home to show off! Huh!"

Well, I couldn't say anything to that; I felt just the same way. It came to me about that time that Espey's claim was the other way. Warren was . . . why, he was walking me home! I didn't know whether to be glad or mad. After all, he hadn't asked me if he could. On the other hand, it was kind of nice to have somebody along.

"I bet old Tyler'll be plenty put out when he comes sparkin' tonight," Warren laughed. "Tyler's really a gone goose. Ma says he's out to marry the teacher an' Pa says it's a doggone shame to have things tore up when we worked so hard to get started. 'Course we can get another teacher—"

That turned me red-headed! I grabbed up a clod and threw it as hard as I could. It didn't hit Warren because I can't throw straight when I'm mad.

"You just hush that talk! We're not going to have any other teacher. We're goin' to have Miss Charity . . . and I hate you to pieces!"

I started running, as fast as I could. Once I looked over my shoulder and Warren was standing right where I'd left him.

Mama was peeling turnips in the kitchen when I got there.

"He said—he said—Tyler was sparkin' Miss Charity —to marry her—an' we'd have some other horrible old teacher—I won't stand for it—I'll never go to that school another day as long as I live!"

"Calm down Betsy," Mama said. "Who said all this?"

"Warren Espey, and I hate him to pieces. I hate his ma and his pa and his mule, Jeems, and the whole state of Indiana where they come from. And it's not the truth, is it? Is it, Mama? Is it?"

Mama put down her knife. "Betsy, I don't know what's going to become of you if you don't stop getting so worked up. The whole state of Indiana! Why, that's where James Whitcomb Riley lives!"

"Well, I don't hate him but I do all the Espeys. Mama, you're just trying to change the subject. Is it true about Miss Charity and Tyler?"

"I'm sure I don't know. It really isn't any of your business. Or the Espeys' business for that matter. But you must understand that a pretty young girl like Charity isn't going on here teaching forever."

"You're with all the rest of 'em, and I hate you, too!" I ran up the stairs and slammed my door. I'd said I hated Mama and I ought to be ashamed because I didn't . . . I didn't. Only one thing for sure, I wasn't going to let Tyler have Miss Charity.

After a while Mama came upstairs and sat down on the edge of our bed. I guess she knew I didn't hate her because she began to rub my back.

"Nell told me about the medal, honey. I'm sorry."

"Gran'ma spelled it that way," I choked, "in my new book."

"I know. Your grandmother never was much of a speller. She didn't get to go to school long because she stayed home to help with the little ones. But she's mighty sweet and she loves you, so don't hold it against her."

"I . . . don't," I said, after a long time. "I know it was really my fault for not studying. I know right where that word is on the page in our speller. Only there it means curly wood stuff for packing. I guess I'll never forget it."

"Then you've gained something. I hope you don't begrudge Elmyra the medal this week. It's about all she has."

I sat up in bed. "Why she has fancier clothes than any of us and fixier lunches and a desk with a back and a gold locket—"

"She doesn't have any friends," Mama said. "Charity told me she was worried about the child, the way Mrs. Stoner pushes her ahead. It's no wonder Elmyra's not happy."

"I'm not very happy, either." I was thinking about

the medal and Miss Charity and Tyler and Warren Espey and all.

"No, you're not now, but in a little while you will be. Remember how Papa used to call you Bouncing Betsy because you'd cry one minute and laugh the next?"

"Yes, ma'am." I tried to hold my face tight to keep from smiling. It seems so wishy-washy not to stay mad. But in about a minute my mouth twitched and I couldn't hold it back.

"That's my girl!" Mama said. "Now get up and wash your face and walk over to Tyler's place and ask him to eat supper with us. That Mr. Grout that's trying to work up the railroad was by here this morning talking to Papa and he left a couple of wild turkey hens he'd shot. I wish to goodness they'd get that railroad or forget about it—keeps Joe stirred up all the time."

"All right," I said, "I'll ask Tyler to eat wild turkey but I'm not going to let him marry Miss Charity. I'm not!"

Mama turned around on me and her eyes snapped. "Betsy, I don't want any foolishness out of you!"

I knew she meant it. Mama can be sweet and wonderful about things like losing the spelling match and saying I hated her, but she wasn't anybody to trifle with. Still, Miss Charity belonged to Skiprock School and I didn't propose to share her with Tyler.

All the way I talked to Rex, pretending he was Tyler, and I got off some real good remarks, only I never can remember them when Tyler's there. And when we got close to the dugout Tyler wasn't in sight. His horse was in the corral and his buggy was outside it so I knew he must be in the dugout, though there wasn't any smoke coming out the stovepipe and it was nearly suppertime.

"Hello the house," I called. "Helloooooooo!"

Nobody answered. Tyler would never in the world go off on foot. Mama teased him about being too bone-lazy to walk. The real reason, he said was that any cowhand that got off his horse in the cattle drive days didn't live to tell about it because longhorns didn't have no respect for a hombre afoot. Thinking about all that I walked up to the dugout door.

The latchstring was hanging out. I don't know why I didn't push the door open. I yelled one more time.

"Hellooooooo!" At first I didn't hear any answer. Then there came a kind of a groan. Rex left me and sniffed at the door.

I gritted my teeth and pushed it open. There was Tyler lying on the dirt floor, so long that he stretched clear across the dugout. And his hand—his left hand— right by the edge of the door so I almost stepped on it . . . covered with blood. His first finger hanging by a piece of skin no mor'n a rag.

"Mama!" I screamed. "Mama, come quick!"

But Mama was back home. There was nobody but me and I had to do something and I didn't know what. A bandage? I looked for a tea towel but Tyler didn't have 'em so I grabbed up my skirt and tried to tear a hunk off my petticoat. It was too stout to tear and I looked for a knife.

There, on the floor beside Tyler, was his hunting knife. He joked about how it was the only household implement he needed, that he shaved, and peeled potatoes, and skinned rabbits, and cobbled boots with it. I picked it up, blood and all, and sliced at my petticoat with it. My good petticoat with the crocheted yoke—pineapple pattern—made by Gran'ma Murdock. That was when I heard Gran'ma's voice, clear as anything, saying, "Soot'll stop bleeding. Cobwebs, too, but soot's handier."

Right then and there I knew it didn't matter that Gran'ma couldn't spell "excelsior."

Thank heavens Tyler's a terrible housekeeper. The stovepipe was shaggy with soot. I scraped it off and squinched my eyes so I could see just a little, and dabbed soot on the cut place. The blood was still coming, still coming. Then I put the finger end in place and I bandaged it as tight as I could. Tight, double tight. Little by little the blood stopped seeping through the layers of muslin.

Then I took the waterbucket and upended it in Tyler's face. He groaned, opened his eyes, shook his head. "Betsy Boy . . . what're you doin'?"

"You big old clumsy!" I yelled, "You cut off your finger, about."

Tyler lifted his hand and looked at the bandage. He winced and gulped. He was so white in the face his freckles looked like they were painted on. "I was . . . slicin' sowbelly for supper. Got to thinkin' 'bout . . . somethin' else . . . somebody else. Reckon I missed my slice."

He rolled over, pulled up his legs and managed to get up to the side of the bunk. "I'm sure obliged to you, Betsy Boy. I guess I fainted. The sight o' blood always did make me sick. Back home I used to run off at hog-killin' time." He looked at me, shamefaced. "I hope this won't . . . get around."

"I'm not a tattletale!"

"Well, I thanky. If you hadn't come along I'd likely've been pushin' daisies instead o' raisin' wheat."

"I didn't want to come. Mama made me. She's got wild turkey for supper and Miss Charity's gone home with Elmyra Stoner and I lost the medal on excelsior and Warren. . . ." The dugout began to whirl around me and the light from the door went black.

The next thing I knew Tyler was pouring water on *me!*

We both heard a wagon rattling and Tyler got the door open and there was Papa! Mama had been worried when I was gone so long. When Tyler told Papa about what happened, Papa rubbed his hand across my wet head and said I was a pretty handy girl to have around in a pinch. You have to know Papa to know what that means!

We were really in luck, because Papa had seen Dr. Motter on the way over and he was going to Thompsons, so Papa turned loose the mustangs and we really hit the high places.

Dr. Motter took Tyler into Thompson's soddy and shooed out the rest of the family, except Mr. Thompson that had a broken leg. He and Tyler came out, finally, smelling of the same smell you get when you pass the saloon in Hardpan.

"Lucky you had medicine with you, Doc," Papa said.

"Medicine's what you got handy," Dr. Motter said. "This little lady, now, she used what was handy and she's saved Tyler's finger. Maybe his life. Maybe he'll live to be hung."

"Now, Doc, don't be hard on a nester," Tyler said. "I'm sure grateful to Betsy. Man needs all his fingers an' toes in this country."

"Well, you'll always have a black line to remind you of the soot, and more'n likely your finger'll be stiff.

Now, I'd better get back to Thompson or my medicine'll all be gone. So long, folks."

Back at our place Miss Charity had come home from Stoners'. When she heard what had happened her eyes got as big as stars. For a terrible minute I thought she was going to hug Tyler! Instead she grabbed and hugged me. I saw myself in the mirror over her shoulder and I was streaked with soot and my hair was wet and stringing down and Miss Charity didn't seem to mind a bit. She went right to her room and got out the box from under the bed and made me a new medal, all my own, that nobody can ever take away from me.

Mama said for me to put the date on it, but instead I marked deep in the soft silver paper, E-X-C-E-L-S-I-O-R!

Everybody laughed but I didn't care. It was my word forevermore. Then Mama gave a little scream.

"Heavenly days! The turkeys!"

She ran to the oven but they were just burned around the edges and we had our own celebration.

Chapter 7

Now that fall plowing and wheat planting were over and cold weather was setting in we had a lot more pupils in Skiprock School. Mama didn't like that one little bit. She said we'd all put our shoulders to the wheel to get things started and now the free riders were piling in. Papa said they paid same as anybody else and she ought to be thankful the neighborhood was getting more educated.

The school committee had to meet to see about getting more seat space. Mr. Espey, Mr. Ryman, and Papa were the committee, but Mrs. Espey, Mrs. Ryman, and Mama did most of the talking. They were meeting at our house and Mama sent Nell and me upstairs. Tom had gone coon hunting with Garvery. Miss Charity was spending the weekend with some friends of her mother's in Alva. I didn't like to have her gone but it meant Tyler wouldn't be around casting sheep's eyes at her for a while.

I hated to admit that Warren was right; still, it looked bad about Tyler. Bad for me and Skiprock School, I mean. I thought up a lot of things to do and all they came to was to get me in trouble with Mama. Like the time I invited Bob Shirk and Tommy Jameson to come over—they were batching it on claims east of ours. I thought that'd discourage Tyler but it just discouraged Bob and Tommy because Tyler came the same night and they had to play checkers all evening while he played his guitar and Miss Charity sang.

Whenever Tyler came I sat in the parlor and looked at the stereopticon. Honestly, I knew those pictures upside down and backwards! That silly one of "Kiss Me First!" just makes me tired. Of course, Mama always came in and told me to go to bed by raising her eyebrows clear up to her hair. Once I pretended not to see what she was doing, but I never tried that again.

Like I said, you can't push Mama around. I did send off for some sneeze powder and when it came I put it in the lapels of Tyler's courting coat that was hanging on a nail in the kitchen. I waited a long time for a sneeze but nothing happened till the next day and Miss Charity sneezed all through school and told everybody she must be coming down with an awful cold!

Nell said I was acting like a great big baby. She thought it was wonderful to have a romance going on at our house. She wrote poetry about it till Papa had to dig out another ledger for her. Well, I didn't care! I mean about what Nell thought. She spent the rest of her time thinking about Shad Ryman, and trying to meet up with him without seeming to. Anyway, she wasn't my boss if she did think she was.

And another thing, if Miss Charity was just *bound and determined* to get married there were rich folks at Alva and Enid that were better prospects. If she married up there she could live in town, have a pump right in the kitchen, and drive around the Square in a fringe-topped surrey. What did Tyler have to offer but a dugout and a half-proved-up claim with a few acres sowed to wheat?

He had True Love, Nell said. She got that dreamy look in her eyes that means she's about to come down with another poem. She scribbled awhile in the new ledger, then she looked up at me.

"What rhymes with 'untarnished'?"

" 'Unvarnished,' " I said. "Plenty of unvarnished stuff at Tyler's claim."

"True Love doesn't care about things like that," Nell said. "Take Lancelot and Guinevere. They didn't care about anything."

"And look at the trouble they caused," I said. I'd read *Idylls of the King* too and I thought a lot of it was pretty silly. "Anyway, Miss Charity's not Queen of King Arthur's Round Table. She's teacher of Skiprock School and she's supposed to stay that."

Nell was hardly listening. "Take John Alden and Priscilla."

"That mealy-mouth! Didn't have gumption to know his own mind!"

"Take Jo March and Professor Bhaer in *Little Women*."

"I always wanted her to marry Laurie."

"Shhhh. The folks are coming in. Wonder if Rymans brought the twins?"

"Boy twins or girl twins?"

"Girls, of course!" Nell pinked up. She couldn't fool me; it was Shad Ryman she wanted to see. Or was it Thad? I got down and put my ear to a crack in the floor.

"No twins at all. Just the grown-ups."

I didn't say that Espeys hadn't brought Warren,

either. No need to get Nell started on that. Not that I cared one way or the other. I had plenty to do with a hem to pick out of my last year's skirt.

I started on the hem. Mama said I was cutting high water with all my skirts and she was going to face every last one of 'em, but picking out a hem's tiresome. I got down on the floor to listen some more.

"Shame on you!" Nell said. "Eavesdroppers hear no good of themselves."

"No, but they hear a lot of other things."

The grown-ups were talking about how could they crowd more benches into the schoolhouse till they could build another. Nobody wanted to build now because pretty soon there'd be school districts and tax money and all. Then it came up that Miss Charity wanted a big map of the United States. Mr. Espey said for what she was being paid she ought to be able to draw one herself. Mrs. Espey said she didn't want Warren learning geography off any hand-drawn map. Mr. Ryman said to hold off till Oklahoma Territory got statehood; then it'd all be changed, anyway.

"I sure wish more words rhymed with 'love'," Nell muttered.

"Mrs. Ryman says we ought to have the schoolhouse floored."

"There's just so much you can do with 'dove' and 'shove.'"

"Papa says a floor would cost like sixty."

Nell tapped her teeth with her pencil:

> *"Oh maiden with the bright gold curls,*
> *Eyes of sapphire, teeth of pearls,*
> *Thy ruby lips do speak of love. . . ."*

"Sounds like a walking jewelry store to me."

"There's always 'heaven above,' " Nell said. "But I've used that."

"Shhhh! They're talkin' about a box social to raise money."

Nell shut the ledger and came down to the floor with me.

"Eavesdropper!"

"This is important. At a box social—well, a lot can happen."

For once Nell was dead right! You never saw an outfit as worked up over anything as Skiprock School was over the box social. The whole neighborhood, too.

I guess you know how a box social's run? Every lady or girl who comes brings a lunch for two in a decorated box. Nobody's supposed to know which box belongs to who . . . whom . . . which. There's an auction sale and the men and boys bid for the boxes. The money goes to the schoolhouse. The lady eats supper with the one that buys her box. It's fun, but it's kind of scary.

Suppose some old married man from out on the salt flats gets your box? Or somebody you just absolutely can't *stand?* Mama says a real lady would never let on that she was disappointed. Besides, it's all in a good cause.

Rymans were to put on the program because they had more talent than any other family, to say nothing of two mandolins, a fiddle, and a mouth organ. Our family was to decorate the schoolhouse. We lived closest of anybody except Gurdys and everybody knew they couldn't do it; besides, Mrs. Gurdy hadn't been seen around for quite some time. Espeys were to provide the extra coal and wood and clean up afterwards because the anti-horse thief bunch was meeting the next night.

Everything was going alone fine till Mrs. Thompson got real mad because Milly hadn't been asked to recite "The Face on the Barroom Floor," with gestures. To keep trouble down Mrs. Ryman put her on the program. Milly shared a bench with me at school and I had to "hear" her old piece about a million times. Milly was very strong on the "with gestures" and when she got to the end where Mr. D'Arcy, the author, has the man to fall down dead, why she just about shoved me onto the floor every time. Then Milly got the measles and that left the program whopperjawed.

Decorating the schoolhouse was hard this time of

year. Mama got Papa and Tom to drive clear to the
Glass Mountains after cedar branches. I found a stand
of buckbrush with red berries on it, and we cut that.
Finally, Mama got out her red sateen petticoat that
she'd had when she was a young lady and cut it into
strips for bows and streamers. I hated to see it go; she
used to let Nell and me play dress-up in it.

Our kitchen smelled good from the wreaths and
ropes we made out of the cedar, even if our hands did
hurt from the prickles. Nell had a bottle of gold paint
and she gilded milkweed pods to put in the wreaths.
The littlest Runninghorse girl brought Miss Charity
some Indian corn and we put that around the blackboard. Meg Orten drew a picture on the blackboard
of Uncle Sam inviting Miss Oklahoma Territory into
the States. Miss Charity wrote, "Welcome Friends,"
in colored chalk over the picture.

On top of all this to-do we had to fix our boxes for
our lunches. Mama said she wouldn't have one, that it
wasn't proper for an old married woman to act so flib-
berty-gibberty. Mrs. Ryman said that was the wrong
spirit. She said she was going to take a box and put a
big piece of persimmon pudding in it in hopes that
Joe Richardson would buy it. *Then she batted her
eyes at Papa.* Papa turned red as a beet and hurried out
to the corral. That put Mama on her mettle. She made
a jam cake with the last jar of blackberry jam.

"It's not that I *care* if you buy Amy Ryman's box," she said to Papa at supper. "I just think the committee should take part. It's all in a good cause."

Papa wasn't paying a bit of attention. "Bert Grout stopped by again. There's a lot more talk about a railroad. Sounds pretty sure this time."

"Railroad'll scare all the game that's left outa the country," Tom said.

"Young man, the country runs on rails! An east-west road through the Strip . . . ."

"You don't need to make a speech," Mama sounded miffed. "I just wonder if Mertons will come to the box social?"

"If Ed thinks it's good for trade, he'll be there with bells on."

"I don't see why you have to put it that way," Mama bristled. "Ed Merton's interested in the good of this community, and this is certainly all in a good cause. Ed's a very fine man."

"Now look here, Louise," Papa was frowning. "I didn't say a word against Ed."

"Ed always did like my jam cake," Mama said. "Even back in Kansas. Even before we were married. Why I remember one Sunday afternoon—"

"I don't see a lick o' sense in buyin' vittles twice," Papa said. "I'd a lot rather give the cash money an' spare you all this work."

"I'm not complaining," Mama said. "It's all in a—"

"—in a good cause," Papa finished. He went outdoors and we could hear him laying down the law to Tom about railroads.

Mama looked at Miss Charity. "Never let a man take you for granted, Charity. Not even after you're married. It's not good for him."

She sliced an apple and laid it over the jam cake and set it in the safe to season. My mouth watered just looking at it but I knew better than to take even a pinch.

Miss Charity's box was covered with blue paper and had silver stars on the sides. She ripped a pink velvet rose off her winter hat and pinned it on top.

"I want that back," she said. "No matter who buys my box, I get the rose."

"You know Tyler'll buy your box if he has to mortgage his claim," Mama said.

"He doesn't have any idea what it looks like. He tried to get me to tell him but I think that's *downright tacky!*"

I think Miss Charity said it so strong because some of the girls at school were actually telling the boys they liked just how they'd decorated their boxes. Or giving very strong hints. I know for a fact that Elmyra Stoner told Fatty Orten that her box was purple with pink ribbons and Fats said that didn't make *him* any mind. He was buyin' on *heft,* not on fancy foofaraw. Jenny Ryman told Trib Carter, I'm positive she did; however else would he know when Jenny's box was decorated exactly like Jeanie's?

Nell's box had gold-painted blackjack leaves glued onto red calico.

"I don't want it too show-offy. Do you think it is, Betsy?"

"Why do you care what I think? You're fixin' it for Shad."

She didn't fly off the handle the way I thought she would. "I wish I was sure that he'd get mine. If anybody else gets it I'll die. Right on the spot."

"Then you'd better tell him which one it is."

"No. You heard what Miss Charity said. Anyway, then he'd know I like him." I just stared at her. "You know what I mean! A girl should never let on that she likes a boy—really likes him—till the right time."

"Who tells you when it's the right time?"

"You'll know when you're older. Is Warren buying your box?"

"I should hope to kiss a pig *not*."

"He asked me how your box was fixed up."

"You'd better not tell him."

Then I told her how it was going to be because she'd know in a little bit anyway. There were some Chicago newspapers left from the stack that we'd used to paper the soddy and I'd cut out all the funny pictures I could find. You know, those about elections and the fat rich man and the skinny poor man and John Bull and Uncle Sam. I figgered to paste those onto the shoebox that my patent-leathered-toed-yellow-silk-stitched slippers had come in.

Nell didn't take to the idea a bit.

"I don't think funny pictures are very—ladylike."

"It'll be different. Nobody'll have one like mine."

"I don't think boys like things different. Too different, that is."

"Boys! All you and Jenny and Jeanie think about is boys!"

Nell put another gold leaf on her box, then she took

it off. "If somebody else would just give Shad a hint!"

"Don't try to pussyfoot around me, Nell, I'm not going to do it."

"If you'd just say a little rhyme I've made up sometime when you're around him. That wouldn't be telling."

"You mean you've already made it up?" She handed me a piece of paper:

> *"Gold and red rings a bell,*
> *Belongs to one I will not tell,*
> *But her name rhymes—well, well, well."*

I burst out laughing. "If that's not tellin' then I never heard it."

"Will you?" Nell begged, "pretty please?"

"Oh, all right. I'll see about it. I've got a good notion to give Tyler a hint since he wants one so bad. Tell him Miss Charity's box is purple and pink. Purple with pink ribbons, la-di-da!"

"But her box is blue and silver," Nell looked puzzled.

"And Elmyra Stoner's is purple and pink. She made purple dye out of pokeberry juice and took the ribbon out of the beading on her petticoat all to catch Fatty Orten. And Fatty won't be caught!"

"I think that's awful!" Nell said, wide-eyed. "To tell Tyler that."

"No awfuller than to tell Shad Ryman. No awfuller

than you." I ran off leaving Nell to stew in her own juice. I didn't really have any idea about telling Tyler wrong, but every now and then it would pop back into my head and make me snicker. Tyler would have a fit. And as for Elmyra—I know you're supposed to love your enemies but she was the hardest one to love I ever have had. Dead set as she was on having Fatty Orten get her box, if it turned out it was Tyler. . . .

Mama called me in and sent me over to Rymans' to borrow the Boston fern to decorate the teacher's desk. Mrs. Ryman was very choice of her Boston fern because it came from Arkansas. She said of course we could borrow the fern—it was all in a good cause—but she'd feel easier in her mind if one of the boys carried it over for me. Neither one was around right now because she'd chased them out. She was making gingerbread cookies and the boys nearly drove her crazy snitching dough before it was baked and she was sure it'd ruin their stomachs but maybe that'd be a blessing in disguise.

She sent Jenny out to round up one of 'em and I ate cookies and talked to Jeanie till they got back. Jenny didn't say if it was Shad or Thad and I felt peculiar about coming out and asking. Nell says Shad's got a scar over his right eyebrow that he got in a duel, only Jenny told me he got it from falling into the churn when he was little. I looked real close and I did see a kind of a scar. Looked more like a seed wart, really.

We walked over to the schoolhouse without hardly a word between us. I was trying so hard to bring Nell's rhyme up kind of natural, that I couldn't think of a thing to say. But how can you be natural about a thing like that? When we got to the schoolhouse I just turned around and blurted out:

> *"Gold and red rings a bell,*
> *Belongs to one I will not tell,*
> *But her name rhymes—well, well, well."*

"How's that?" Shad blinked. He rubbed his hand over his forehead, pushed back his stocking cap and scratched his head. "Come again, please?"

I said it again but I didn't finish because right in the middle I saw that the scar was gone! My jaw dropped. It'd been nothing but a little dollop of raw cookie dough he'd snitched off the bread board and rubbed away just now! I felt terrible!

I tried to explain that in case he was Thad he was to tell the rhyme to Shad only not to tell him that I told him, and especially not to tell Nell that I told him to tell him . . . . Oh, it was a mess.

" 'Gold and red,' " he grinned. "Well, I reckon that's a tip I c'n use." He walked off whistling, his hands in his pockets.

I was in the soup!

I went right home and told Nell and she cried and said I'd ruined her life and she was sure I'd done it on purpose and she'd never forgive me in a thousand years.

There was one good thing. She couldn't tattle to Mama!

I went on downstairs where Miss Charity was trying on the new dress Cousin Marcy had sent for the box social. It was a blue wool challis, just the color of her eyes, made with a tight basque, a backdraped skirt, leg of mutton sleeves buttoned into long tight cuffs. I watched her turn around to check the hemlines.

"If a person married a rich person a person could wear dresses like that all the time," I said.

"Money isn't everything. Remember the story of King Midas in our Reader?"

"I wonder if that's too short?" Mama said.

"I wouldn't want my ankles to show," Miss Charity said.

"When I get married it's going to be somebody rich and handsome."

"I thought you didn't like boys," Mama said. "The way you act to that nice little Espey boy—"

Nice little! Who wants to be called that?

"Sometimes I like 'em and sometimes I don't. I'd rather be a schoolteacher like Miss Charity. That's the nicest thing in the world."

Miss Charity reached over and hugged me. "You'd be a fine teacher, Betsy, but would you want to teach all your life?"

"I don't know why not? Why would I want to change?"

"You might like something else better. After a while."

I walked away from Miss Charity and got Mama's shawl from the hook by the door and went out down by the old soddy. The edges of the sod "bricks" were all rounded now. Even the soddy was changing. Well, I didn't like changes! And I wasn't going to let any happen at Skiprock School. Not if I could help it.

And just as if I'd brought him up by black magic Tyler Evans came riding by on the road. I waved and he stopped and I ambled out as if I didn't have a thing in the world on my mind.

We passed the time of day, innocent as a couple of spring lambs, then Tyler took out his makings and rolled a cigarette.

"You folks all set for the big box social?"

"We've got our boxes decorated but Mama won't fix the lunches till tomorrow."

"How 'bout givin' a fellow a hint about you-know-whose?"

"Why Tyler!" I acted shocked. "That'd be down-right tacky!"

"Aw no. Not when you'n' me're pardners. Why I'm wearin' yore brand, Betsy Boy." He held up his finger with the black soot mark circling the end.

"Well," I said, "I guess I can give you a *hint*. Now you listen. . . .

> *Purple and pink, purple and pink,*
> *Those are the prettiest colors I think.*"

I guess Nell's not the only one in our family that can make up rhymes! Tyler swallowed it, hook, line, and sinker. He thanked me, gave me a piece of gum and rode off singing, *"As I went down to Laredo, Laredo, As I went down to Laredo one day. . . ."*

When I got over laughing I felt kind of weasly. I put the gum in my pocket instead of chewing it. But when you came right down to it, was I to blame if Tyler thought I was talking about Miss Charity's box? He hadn't said her name, and neither had I. I'd just said I liked purple and pink. Besides, he didn't have any business coming around asking me something I wasn't supposed to tell.

Next night was the box social. School let out early so that Mama could put up the decorations. Miss Charity stayed to help Mama. Everybody was whispering and giggling and swapping secrets. Everybody but me. I wished the whole thing was over and done with.

When we started home after Miss Charity chased us away from the window, I watched Warren Espey cut Nell out of her bunch like a cutting horse working a herd of cows. I knew he was going to ask her what my box was like. That silly funny picture idea. Why had I ever done such a thing? It was too late to change now. Mama had packed the lunch in all four of our boxes and brought them to the schoolhouse with the decorations.

Nell and Tom were going to Ryman's for supper and all of 'em going to the box social together. Jenny invited me, too, but I knew it was only for politeness and I didn't think I could stand to listen to all that giggling and going on about who was going to buy what box. I said I thanked her kindly but I'd go with Mama and Papa and Miss Charity in the wagon.

That was another thing. Tyler growled like a bear

with a sore paw when Miss Charity wouldn't go with him in his buggy. She said that this was a school affair and she couldn't show favoritism. My, but he was put out!

I walked on home, getting slower and slower. I hustled up some when I saw a strange team and buckboard at the gate and Papa standing there with one foot in the rig.

"Hurry up, Betsy!" Papa called. "I got to be on my way."

When I got closer I saw that it was Mr. Grout in the buckboard and he was holding the team with his feet braced.

"Where you goin', Papa?"

"Goin' in to Hardpan with Grout to a meetin' about the railroad. Tell your Mama to expect me when she sees me."

"But—it's the box social."

"Can't be helped. This won't wait." Then Papa laughed, kind of sour. "Maybe Ed Merton'll buy your Mama's box. I'm leavin' the team and wagon for you folks. Tell Tom not to run the mustangs." Papa was in the buckboard.

"Tom's gone to Ryman's," I called but Mr. Grout gave the team their heads and off they went on the road to Hardpan.

I went on into the house. It was cold and drafty. I

wished we had our good old warm soddy back. I slumped down in a chair and just sat there staring at all the mess Mama had left from packing the lunches. I sat there and sniffled and coughed and tried not to think about tonight.

When Mama and Miss Charity got home I was still sitting there. I told them about Papa, and Mama was fit to be tied. Then all of a sudden she turned around on me, like it was my fault!

"And you! Sitting here doing nothing with all these dirty dishes and all the extra work I've got to do! The very least you could have done—"

"I'll wash the dishes and Betsy can dry," Miss Charity was tying on an apron. I was too miserable to thank her, except with my eyes. She shook her head and put her finger on her lips and started dipping hot water out of the reservoir on the back of the stove.

"I guess we'll just have to pitch in," Mama was scolding. "And a good thing we've got no menfolks to feed. We can make-do for supper. We'll have to walk to the schoolhouse, besides. I wouldn't touch that mustang team with a forty-foot pole. How on earth we'll get home—"

"Tyler will bring us," Miss Charity dipped up soft soap.

"I won't step my foot in his buggy," I said.

"One more word out of you, young lady, and you

won't go at all!" Mama grabbed up the bucket and went
out to milk Old Blue.

"I wish you didn't feel this way about Tyler," Miss
Charity handed me a plate to dry. "He thinks a lot of
you."

"He's the hatefulest—aggravatin'est—" Smash! The
plate hit the floor. It was one that had come from Kansas buried in flour. "And just look what he made me
do!"

"Don't cry, Betsy. It was an accident." Miss Charity
was down helping me pick up the pieces.

"I am *not* crying!" I swiped my sleeve along my
eyes and nose. "I think I've got the nervous prostra-
tion." That was the disease Cousin Merthula had and
everybody had to do just what she wanted 'em to all
the time.

Miss Charity's mouth twitched. "We're all feeling
kind of—strung up. I, for one, will be glad when this
box social is over and we can get back to our regular
school work."

"What would you do if somebody else—not Tyler—
got your box?"

"Why—nothing. I'd be sorry but I don't see how I
could do anything! After all, it's all in a good cause.
But what made you ask, Betsy?"

Miss Charity's arm was warm and soft across my
shoulders.

"Please don't go off and get married," I whispered. "I don't want anybody but you to teach at Skiprock School. Not ever."

"I can't make a promise like that," Miss Charity said, "but I'll make you another one. If anybody in the Strip asks me to marry him, I'll tell you about it, the very first person."

It wasn't much of a promise, but it did mean that Tyler hadn't asked her yet and if things went my way at the box social, maybe they'd have a big fuss or something.

We finished the dishes and set out cold supper. Mama came in, still mad as a wet hen, and we ate—though I didn't hardly taste a thing—and then there were the dishes *again*. Honestly, I think that on the Day of Judgment Mama'll make us stop and do dishes. The stove was crowded with water heating for baths.

Mama dragged out the tin tub and dumped in the hot water. "By the time Betsy's done washing, the water'll be warm for you, Charity. Betsy, for heaven's sake stop staring and get a hustle on!"

I came up and put my hand in the water to see if it was too hot or too cold. All at once Mama looked at me as if she hadn't seen me in a week. She squinted, sniffed, whirled me around, and lifted my braids.

"What's wrong? Is my neck dirty? Do I have . . . nits?"

Mama put her arms around me and all the madness and crossness was gone out of her. "Betsy, honey, you've got—the measles."

"Ohhhhhh nooooooo!"

"I should have known," she said to Miss Charity. "But I've been so busy. That cough, and that drippy nose—but it took that old measles smell to tell me. See the rash in the edge of her hair?"

"Milly Thompson came down last week. They share a bench at school."

"I'll never speak to that hateful girl as long as I live!"

"Hush, Betsy, you know it's not her fault. I just wish I'd put you to bed with Nell when she got 'em but I sent you to Gran'ma's. Now—this settles the box social. You and I will stay home."

"I don't see why. I was at school today and nobody will know—"

"I know," Mama said, "and that's a-plenty. Anyway, measles are tricky. They can go hard if you're not careful at first. Now stop that crying or you'll hurt your eyes."

"I'll bring you part of my lunch," Miss Charity said. "And no matter how late it is I promise I'll wake you up and tell you all about it."

"And I'll read to you, as long as you want and whatever you want," Mama said.

They made a big fuss over me, fixed up a bed in the

corner of the kitchen out of chairs and quilts and brought me drinks of water. Miss Charity lugged the tin tub into Mama's room and had her bath and came out all dressed in the blue wool challis. I never saw anybody as pretty and I guess I never will.

"I hate to have you walk over by yourself, Charity," Mama worried. "There'll be a moon, and you can take the lantern. If we could just get a-hold of Tyler—"

"Don't worry, Cousin Louise. I'm not afraid. He'll bring me home."

"Maybe he won't," I said. "Maybe he'll be mad—about something."

They both turned around, surprised, and stared at me. I wished I could have crawled in a hole and pulled it in after me. Then all three of us heard the sound of running feet pounding toward our house. Mama's eyes flickered to the empty place where Papa's gun stayed before Skip Rentner took it.

"Miz Richardson—please—Miz Richardson—."

Mama opened the door. Garvery Gurdy stumbled in. His face was as near white as it could be and his eyes behind that straggly mess of black hair shone with being scared. He was panting so hard he couldn't talk.

"Garvery! You gave me a turn." Mama had her hand on her throat. "What's wrong?"

Garvery hung onto the door frame as if his life depended on it. "Miz Richardson—please come quick—

it's Ma—she's took bad—she told me to come git you—
please come!"

"What's wrong? What's the matter?"

Garvery just said it all over again.

"But Betsy's got the measles and Charity's due at
the schoolhouse—"

"Ma said you'd come," Garvery said. "She said you
would."

Then Miss Charity touched Mama on the arm. "Go
ahead, Cousin Louise. I'll stay with Betsy."

"Ma said none of the others thought she was good
enough to visit with, even. But you'd been nice. She's—
she's took *bad*."

"Charity, it's the box social and you're the teacher—"

"Some things are more important than box socials"
—Miss Charity smiled in a kind of watery way—
"though I'll admit it didn't seem like it this afternoon.
You go on and I'll stay right here."

Mama put her hands to her head. "What a day!
Serves me right for getting Joe all aggravated! Now,
let me see. . . . Garvery, when did your mother take
down?"

"Two-three hours back. Mebbe more. I dunno. I
wasn't t'home."

"All right. You start for home now. I'll be there as
quick as I can round up some things and hitch. Maybe
I'll pick you up along the way. Scoot!"

Garvery was out of the door like a shot.

"Mama," I said, "it's the mustang team."

"I know," Mama said, "but the Lord helps you to do what you have to do. I can get there quicker this way and I think Mrs. Gurdy needs me *now*. I'll hitch. Charity, get some things together for me. Betsy—you pray."

Well, we did it. Miss Charity flew around, her blue wool challis skirt following her like a kite in a high wind. She grabbed the flannel Mama was using to face my skirt, the muslin for Nell's new underdrawers. She folded the Rose and Ring quilt from her bed around those things. She took all the cooked food out of the safe—even the last of the jam cake that hadn't gone in the box lunches.

All I could think of to say was, "Lord, take care of Mama. *Lord, take care of Mama!*" Maybe I should have thought about Mrs. Gurdy, too, but I didn't. I just said it over and over.

Mama came back into the house with her mouth in a thin straight line, her hair tumbling out of its pins and dust streaking her long coat. She was carrying the lighted lantern.

"Hurry! They won't stand."

Miss Charity handed her the things. "I put in some food."

"Good. It'll come in handy."

"Don't worry about Betsy and me."

"Don't worry about Miss Charity and me."

We said it at the same time so that it was all mixed together.

"I'm not worried," Mama said. "I know one thing for sure and certain—*I can depend on my family!*"

She kissed both of us and then she was gone.

We listened to the sound of Mama's voice, talking down the team. Then there was a rattle and roll of wheels and from the direction of the noise we knew Mama had taken the mustangs straight 'cross country.

Lord! Take care of Mama!

I don't know whether I said it out loud or not but Miss Charity came over and smiled at me and said, "He will, Betsy. I know He will."

"Now let me get out of this dress and we'll make some molasses taffy. I've heard that's very good for the measles!"

I unhooked the back of the blue wool challis. It felt as soft as a kitten's ear. About the middle of the back I couldn't stand it any longer.

"I—I told Tyler your box was purple and pink— that's Elmyra's—I didn't out-and-out tell him. I only kind of let him think the wrong thing."

"That's just the same," Miss Charity said.

"I know. I shouldn't've."

"But—Elmyra Stoner!" Miss Charity plunked down in the kitchen rocker. "Why Elmyra?"

"Oh, she's dead stuck on Fatty Orten. I thought I could—could—"

"Kill two birds with one stone?"

"Yes ma'am," I nodded. Then I thought of something. "Maybe the measles is punishment for what I did!"

"You'd have had the measles, box social or no box social. Stop trying to make yourself into something special."

It was the first time she'd ever sounded real cross with me. I guess—I guess I didn't blame her. When I started all this I just thought about giving Tyler a bad turn; now I saw how it'd seem to Miss Charity. I mean having Tyler not even bid on her box when it came up and somebody awful getting it, maybe. Things turn out different than you think they're going to.

"I'm—I'm sorry," I said, real low.

She heard me and looked over and smiled. Then she began to laugh.

"Cousin Louise told me—never let a man—take you for granted—I guess this'll—settle Mr. Evans' hash!"

She went on laughing and I laughed, too. I wasn't sure just why we were laughing but I knew you don't laugh that way with people you're down-deep mad at.

Miss Charity made the taffy then and poured it on the ironstone platter to cool. She got out *Lorna Doone* and began to read. After awhile we pulled the taffy and snipped it into pieces and I got a hunk stuck in my back teeth, and so did Miss Charity, and that made her reading sound funny, so we laughed a lot more.

In the middle of the third chapter we heard a buggy coming down the road. We both knew who it was. Tyler Evans, and no mistake. I'd just as well admit I was scared to face him. If I hadn't had the measles I'd have run off and hidden. I must have showed what I was thinking for Miss Charity told me to lie still and keep covered.

"I'll handle this," she said. "It's partly my problem."

Now I know what authors mean by "quaked in his boots," only I quaked in my quilts. After a long, long time the door opened and they came in. I wanted to pull the covers over my head but I was too ashamed to hide! Tyler came over to me and stood there.

"Well, Betsy Boy, the teacher's been givin' me a real lecture. Seems like I didn't have any business askin' you for secret information. And she says it serves me right that I got it wrong."

"Now, Tyler," Miss Charity said, "don't misquote me."

"Anyway, it looks like you 'n' me both got our signs crossed, Betsy Boy. How 'bout forgettin' it an' startin' over?"

"Yessir," I said, and it was the first time I'd ever said "sir" to Tyler.

"All's well that ends well," he said. "The box social was a big fi-nancial success. Mrs. Ryman said the take'd come to around $20. The box that brought the most money was blue with silver stars and a pink velvet rose a-top it. Ed Merton bought it. Said he had a nose like a bluetick hound for jam cake. Said he was sorry there wasn't no lady to go with the box, but it doubled his ration of cake."

Tyler pulled something out of his pocket.

"My rose!" Miss Charity gasped. "I'd given out ever seeing it."

"*Your* rose? Well, I reckon I'll have to give it to you. Ed gave it to me and said I was to give it to some pretty

girl as he didn't fancy his wife's finding it in his pocket."
Tyler stuck the rose behind Miss Charity's ear, and
she snatched it away, *and batted her eyes at him.* (I
guess that's something I'm going to have to learn to do,
but it sure looks *silly.*)

"Who got Nell's box?" I asked.

"One of the Ryman boys. Couldn't say which."

"Who got Cousin Louise's?"

"That little tub o' lard of Ortens'. That kid's a cau-
tion. Eats like he never saw food before and don't expect to again."

"Whose box did you get?" Miss Charity asked.

"The box of the girl that's the tore-downdest speller
in Skiprock School. She told me so herself. But her ma's
not the cook Miss Louise is."

"If that's a hint," Miss Charity said, "it won't do you
a bit of good. We sent all the food with Cousin Louise
and all there is here is taffy. But I'll make up a pot of
coffee to go with it."

"I c'n do better'n that," Tyler said, and left and went
out to his buggy. He'd told us all that we'd asked about
the box social, but the one thing I couldn't ask was,
"Who got my box?" I wanted to know real bad, but it
stuck in my throat. I wished Miss Charity would ask
but I felt meechy about bringing it up. Would it be
Wormy McFadden? Ugh! Or Elmo John Jones? Double
ugh! Or some old tobacco-chewing man?

Tyler came back inside, and in his big freckled hand was my box! My very own box, all covered with funny pictures.

"Didn't—didn't—anybody buy it?"

"Sure thing! That curley-haired Espey boy. Walter? Warner? Willipus-wallipus?"

"You know good and well his name's Warren!"

"That's right, so it is. Well, it seems he bought this box thinkin' some girl went with it and he was mighty down-in-the-mouth when he found out he'd paid six bits to eat by himself."

"Six bits! Why—that's seventy-five cents!"

"Sure is. The biddin' went high on account of all the funny pictures. Well, when I saw how he felt—and feelin' pretty much the same way m'self—I offered him eighty cents. He took it, providin' I'd tell you he sure wanted those pictures and he knew it was yours because you were the only girl in Skiprock School smart enough to deck a box like that."

"Did he? Really?" Tyler nodded. "Tyler, I thank you—I thank you very kindly."

"Don't mention it," he said. "We're pardners."

We divided up the box lunch and there was plenty because Mama always provides with a lavish hand. Even plenty of jam cake. The light began to hurt my eyes so Miss Charity turned out the lamp and we sat in the moonlight. Tyler got his guitar and played cowboy songs.

> *As I rode down to Laredo, Laredo,*
> *As I rode down to Laredo one day,*
> *I saw a young cowboy all dressed in white linen,*
> *All dressed in white linen and cold as the clay. . . .*

Miss Charity thought that one was too sad so he sang "The Strawberry Roan," and started on "San Antonio," and I couldn't hold my eyes open any longer.

But I did hear Tyler hitch his chair over closer to Miss Charity. I wasn't *that* sleepy.

Chapter 8

*M*easles are no joke. I was so sick that I didn't care if school kept or not. I couldn't read. I couldn't write—not even to put things down for my book. I couldn't stand the taste of anything to eat— it was all like brass. I itched and itched and itched and taking soda water sponge baths didn't help nearly as much as Mama said it did.

Part of the time I wanted to be let alone. Part of the time I wanted someone there. Only nobody knew which part I wanted when, not even me. Mama said she'd have gone stark raving crazy if it hadn't been for Miss Charity.

Every day Miss Charity came right home from school and read to me and told me all about what happened at recess. She didn't go any place at night or even have company. My measles did a lot more to keep her and Tyler apart than any of my other plans. But a person can't go on having the measles for years and years. I was going to have to think up something else.

When Nell came home from Rymans' the morning after the box social you'd never guess what! She was crazy about *Thad*. He had bought her box and she said he was handsomer than Shad and smarter, too, and she now thought he was the one she'd liked all the time. She gave me her blue hair ribbon because I'd told Thad about her box instead of Shad. Before, she'd been ready to have me ground up into sausage meat for doing the same thing. Figger that out!

I had plenty of chance to talk to Nell because Mama didn't get home from Gurdys' for three days. Papa walked over, early, and brought back the team and the word that Gurdys had a new baby girl and Mama said we must all do the best we could and for Nell to make some catnip tea with a pinch of tansy in it and give it to me to break me out good. Nell made it too strong and it tasted so awful I thought she was trying to poison me so I poured it into the Joseph's Coat plant and it died and I guess that shows you.

By the afternoon of the third day Mama'd been gone

I was back in our room and Nell and I were pretty tired of each other. I didn't see why any old baby—even if it was a new baby—needed Mama more than I did. Nell promised that if I'd quit being so cranky she'd show me something. Only I had to promise never, never, never to tell Mama. Or Miss Charity. Or Gran'ma Murdock.

She closed our bedroom door, then she pulled back the blanket that was hung at the window to keep the light out of my eyes and peeked out as if old Geronimo might come galloping up, any minute. She lighted our lamp and turned the wick down low and took the top drawer out of our dresser and reached into the space behind and pulled out a pamphlet kind of thing, printed on pink paper. I'd been sitting up, watching, and I flopped back down into the covers.

"Whatever in the world's so secret about an old paper?"

"This isn't just any old paper. It's one where you can get a husband or a wife."

"You mean order, like ordering from the catalogue?"

"No silly. First you write a letter and tell about yourself. You know—that you're pretty, over twenty-one, have money in the bank, you're a hard worker, and you love children. . . . All like that."

"I never heard of such a thing."

"Then you send a dollar and the letter and they

print it and somebody reads it and sends another dollar to the paper and gets your address and then you write each other and then—"

"That's a lot of money. Two dollars."

"Not for a husband—I guess. Or a wife."

"Let me see the paper."

There it was, letter after letter.

"Jenny Ryman got it from her cousin that lives in Chicago. Her cousin knew, actually knew, a girl that knew a girl that got a husband this way. And they lived happy ever after."

"Ever after?"

"As long as this girl that knew this girl heard anything about 'em."

"Are you going to write a letter?"

Nell grabbed the paper out of my hand. "The very idea! Of course not. Besides, I don't have a dollar."

"Give it back. I want to read all the letters."

"You might hurt your eyes." Nell turned out the lamp. "Anyway, you're too young for such things."

I threw my pillow at her and she threw it right back at me. We had to stop our pillow fight because Papa came in and said that Garvery had brought word that Mama was ready to come home. Nell scurried around, trying to get the house slicked up and forgot to hide the paper. I got it and hid it myself, under the corn-shuck mattress.

When Mama got home she sat by my bed and talked about the new baby all the time, hardly noticing how sick I was.

"What's her name?" I said, "If she's all that fancy."

"They only named her this morning."

"Bet it's something awful like Goldilocks Aspidistra."

Mama's eyebrows went 'way up. "The baby's name is Louise Betsy. Louise for me and Betsy for you. Mrs. Gurdy said she hoped the baby would grow up to be a nice, sweet girl *just like you.*"

I could have crawled under a peanut shell. It was the very first time I'd had a baby named after me. It makes you stop and think. I decided I'd try to act more lady-like and be a good example. Then I remembered how little she was and I was glad I wouldn't have to start right away. As soon as she got big enough to notice I'd change off.

Mrs. Ryman came over to bring some wild grape jelly to me, special, because I had the measles. She came right out and asked Mama how she *stood* three days at Gurdys'.

"They may not do things our way, Amy, but you couldn't help feeling different if you saw how they love that baby."

"Whit Gurdy? I didn't suppose he'd notice, hardly."

"Oh, I'll admit I had to souse his head in the water

bucket to bring him 'round when I first got there, but after that—why, he couldn't do enough. And Garvery —why he thinks she's the sweetest—cutest—prettiest—"

"Did he *say* so?"

"Now, Amy, you know Garvery won't talk unless he has to. But just the way he looks at her, and holds her —it's—it's downright touching." Mama wiped her eyes. "I tell you, I'll never run down Gurdys again."

When she said that, Mama gave Mrs. Ryman a look that said, same as words, "And you'd better not do it when I hear you, either."

From that time on Gurdys were our friends. As soon as I got over the measles Mama took me over to see the

baby. And it was true, just what she said Garvery thought. Louise Betsy was the sweetest . . . cutest . . . prettiest . . . She had big blue eyes and brown curls and she let me hold her and love her and I was the first one she smiled for.

Winter went rolling along, going uphill till Christmas, then downhill till Easter. It doesn't show that on the calendar but I think of it that way.

We didn't have what you'd call a big Christmas. Nobody in the Strip had really made a crop yet. All of us were the same—not poor, we just didn't have any money.

All our family got presents. I got a heart-shaped pincushion made from some red sateen Mama had saved back from the petticoat and my initials on it in black-headed pins. Nell knitted Tom and me mittens—his too small and mine too big. Tom found a pecan tree and got a sack of nuts for all of us. I took my Roman-striped hair ribbon and made bookmarkers with embroidered mottoes on them. (Nell put hers in her ledger of poems so I *know* she liked it.) Papa gave each one of us an orange. Miss Charity gave our whole family a green copy of *Lamb's Tales from Shakespeare* and promised to read it out loud. Tyler gave her a pink celluloid comb and brush set in a red satin box, and she knitted him some sleeve garters.

There *was* one other thing, if I'm going to tell all the truth. Christmas night an orange turned up on our front steps with my initials cut out of the skin. Nobody in our family believes that I do *not* know who it was from. All I have to say is that if Warren Espey can't put his name on presents, he'll get no thanks from me. Two oranges in one day! That's really living high on the hog.

By Easter things were tighter than at Christmas. There wasn't any talk about new dresses; we were lucky to have old ones. Brother Simmons preached at Skiprock School in the afternoon and came home with us to supper. Mama had held back a half-dozen eggs out of those she traded at the store and she boiled them in beet juice and put one at each place on blue glass butter chips.

In the late Spring Gran'ma Murdock sent us a big box. When things got real bad Gran'ma seemed to know it and along came something nice. That's kind of funny, too, because she was dead set against our coming to the Strip. She carried on terrible and said she was going to pray every night for Joe to see the error of his ways. Papa bristled up at that and Mama had to smooth him down and Gran'pa had to get smelling salts for Gran'ma. . . . Oh, it was a mess.

Still, Gran'ma was the one who sent us things. Good things to eat, quilts, dresses, books, slates and slate pen-

cils, rolls of Kansas newspapers. Why, she even sent
Louise Betsy a baby dress with six rows of tucking, and
a scalloped flannel sacque. Mama let me take it over
and Mrs. Gurdy cried and said it was the nicest thing
that she'd ever heard of and she'd not forget it, not to
her dying day, and she hoped my Gran'ma would come
to the Strip so she could tell her herself. I said I hoped
Gran'ma would come, too, but I didn't tell Mrs. Gurdy
that she'd have had a double-duck conniption fit at
the way their soddy looked. Louise Betsy was cooing
and smiling so it was plain that *she* didn't mind and I
guess what Gran'ma doesn't know won't hurt her.

This was the year that Papa and Tyler had real
hopes of a wheat crop. Land in the Strip is the best
wheat land in the world. I've heard plenty of menfolks,
besides Papa, say that. Of course it hadn't been plowed
before the Run so it took a lot of hard work to get it
ready. Mr. Gurdy wouldn't even try. He said the Wheat
Trust had the market cornered and by the time a person made a crop it wouldn't be worth harvesting. Papa
said he was glad that he wasn't that far-sighted and he
figgered folks'd always have a need for flour, if only
for the ladies to powder their noses.

He and Tyler kept right on working and Tom
worked with them whenever he wasn't in school. Tyler
was quieter than he used to be. He didn't haul on my
braids, or yarn to Tom. Mama said he was worrying

over the crop and holding off asking Miss Charity to
marry him till he had something ahead.

That sure put me between a rock and a hard place!

Our crop and Tyler's were right spang up together,
except for the old road, left from the cattle drive days.
If we made a good crop, Tyler did. And if he made a
good crop Miss Charity would more than likely marry
him and Skiprock School was out in the cold with a
new teacher that I was sure would be somebody I dee-
spised. On the other hand, if Tyler didn't make a good
crop then we didn't either and there wouldn't be
money enough to buy groceries, let alone go to school,
and Miss Charity'd have to go back to Kansas. I knew
this because I heard Papa and Mama talking about it.

"If it comes right down to it, we can always go back
home," Papa said. "I can get a job working for somebody . . . I guess."

"We're not going crawling home." Mama thumped
the dough she was kneading. "If we don't make a crop
this year, we will next."

It was quiet; then Papa cleared his throat.

"Louise—we've got less'n five dollars cash."

"We've got credit. We've always paid our bills and
Ed Merton knows it."

"Yes, but . . . I kind of hate to ask Ed."

"I know. But it won't be as if you were the only one.
He's got half the county on his books."

"Well, we'll see. Just tough it out a day at a time."

"That's all the Lord gives us," Mama said. "I'm willing to trust Him."

"I trust the Lord and you," Papa said, "but dogged if I trust the weather. Ever since we got to the Strip it's been so dry a feller has to be primed to spit. Now we've got a little rain—but, I don't know. I don't know."

As the weather settled into Spring, Skiprock School got smaller and smaller. All the big boys that came in the winter dropped out to help in the fields. Then the girls began to drop out but mostly that was because money was too tight to pay their dollar a month. School was down to a few squirmy little kids and our family . . . we didn't have to pay cash because we boarded Miss Charity. Shad and Thad quit in March and in April Jenny and Jeanie brought a note saying that their mother was arranging for "private instruction at home." Miss Charity's feelings were hurt about that till Mama explained that Mrs. Ryman was from the South and she just couldn't bear to come out and say she couldn't send the two dollars. Warren Espey quit in April, too. At least I wouldn't have to be bothered with *him*. Elmyra Stoner hung on like the blackjack leaves in the springtime.

At the end of April Miss Charity told Papa to tell the committee that she thought it best to close the

school for awhile and start another term after harvest. She started packing to go back to Kansas and I saw her crying and wiping her eyes on her rolled-up lisle stockings.

Nell said it was on account of Tyler. That he was letting her go back to Kansas without saying a word about getting married. Mama scolded Nell; I mean for blaming Tyler.

"An honorable man doesn't propose until he can name the date. Tyler can't ask Charity to marry him when he's not sure whether he can provide for her or not. He's waiting to see about this crop. . . ."

It looked as if everything in the world depended on the crop, and the crop depended on the weather.

To know a wheat crop you have to go along with it all the way. In the Strip the sod had to be turned over first and left to kill the grass roots. The long rows of

turned-over sod were clean and shining in the sun.
Maybe it sounds peculiar to say that dirt is clean, but
I think new-plowed dirt's the cleanest thing I know of.
Papa ran a harrow over the dirt to break up the big
clods and then came the part I liked the best. Sowing
the wheat.

Our seed-wheat came from Kansas. Pushing your
arms clear to the elbow in wheat grains is like dipping
them into cool water, then coming up with your fists
full of wheat is the same as holding water in your
hands and letting it trickle through your fingers. Of
course, I always sneaked out a little to chew. Wheat
makes a kind of nutty-tasting chewing gum, if you
work on it long enough and your teeth are good
enough. But all that was just kid-stuff. The real thing
came when Papa slung a bag around his neck and
broadcast the wheat in the harrowed field. Some folks

had a drill, but they cost money and Papa said he could
still sling a curve. All our family went out to watch
that first day and Mama and Nell and I sang:

> *"We plow the fields and scatter*
> *The good seed on the land,*
> *But it is fed and water'd*
> *By God's almighty hand. . . ."*

The birds came from nowhere, swooping, twittering,
and singing. Long, wiggly fishworms worked in the
dirt around our feet. A big old jackrabbit went loping
across the field, stopping every now and then to look
at us and down at the dirt as if he'd never seen a plowed
patch in his life . . . and maybe he hadn't. Rex ran
after the birds, barking, and across the road Tyler was
sowing wheat, too, trying to do it just like Papa. Papa
quit and called him over.

"Tyler, you make me nervous wasting seed that-a-
way. You're goin' to have a field as patchy as a scalp
with the barber's itch."

"Joe! Watch your language," Mama said.

"If I could do it on horseback," Tyler said, "I think
I'd do better. I get uneasy afoot."

"Hold off till tomorrow. I'll come over and give you
a hand."

"And I'll mend up that harness of yours. It's kinda
patchy."

After the sowing, Papa and Tom made a drag of wild plum bushes and put it behind the team and dragged the field to cover the seed-wheat. Then came the waiting. Farming has a lot of waiting in it. This year we got a real rain. My, how the wheat pushed up . . . as if it couldn't wait to get above ground. I thought that was fine, but, sure enough, Papa started to worry again.

"Oughta be pastured down. Let wheat get high enough to hide a jackrabbit and you'll never make a crop."

We turned Old Blue and the mustang team on the wheat. Mama even carried her little pen of chickens out. Then Papa worried that the stock would get too much green stuff.

And just in time we got a good snow.

When Springtime came the wheat waked up and stretched and remembered about growing again. As it grew higher and the weather got warmer I loved to go out and stand on the old cattle drive road that divided our place from Tyler's. All around was green . . . green . . . green. . . . Every breath of wind rippled the green and changed its shade till I was dizzy with looking. I wished, I wished that I could dive into the wheat and let it hold me up and swim through it.

Of course I didn't try. I could ruin a whole bushel doing a silly thing like that. But I *wished* I could.

When wheat gets close to cutting time, a man that has a good stand holds his breath . . . and so does his family. Every morning after the wheat showed gold instead of green our whole family looked at the sky, first thing in the morning. We never said *why;* it was too important to talk about. So many weather things can ruin a crop. Rain. Hail. Lightning. A bad windstorm can whip ripe wheat down so that it can't be cut.

After Miss Charity went back to Kansas I walked to the field with Papa in the morning. He'd pick a head of wheat, pull it apart, stare at the grains, rub them with his thumb, pull his moustache, then finally he'd flip the head of wheat back into the field and put his hand down on my hair. He'd stroke my hair kind of absent-mindedly, and whistle "Sam Bass" under his breath, rocking on his heels. We were standing that way one morning when Tyler came up the road.

"Whaddya think, Joe? Whaddya think?"

"Looks good. Up to now. Considerin'. . . ." Papa said.

"When'll it be ready for harvest?"

"Couldn't say. There's milk left in the kernel yet. Don't want to get ahead of ourselves an' we don't want the weather to get ahead of us." Papa gazed at the sky.

Tyler pulled my left braid, kind of half-heartedly. "And your mama don't believe in gamblin', Betsy Boy. Wonder what she thinks a farmer does?"

Not long after that Mama had a letter from Miss Charity. She said she was downright homesick to see us and she asked all manner of questions about everybody in the neighborhood—except Tyler. That tickled me. I thought it meant she'd forgotten him. Nell said I was absolutely and entirely wrong. It meant that she loved him so much she couldn't stand to ask about him. I thought about the wheat crop and how we all watched the weather without a word and I decided Nell might be right. I decided it in my mind; I didn't tell Nell.

It was high time I did something to separate those two for good and all. For better or worse. Something desperate.

Did you ever notice that when you decide to do something, more than likely you'll get a shove, one way or the other? Well. Mama called me to stop mooning around and go bring in the wash and sort out the clothes, not dump 'em down the way I usually did.

My everyday petticoat made from bleached sacks trimmed with feather-stitching had a three-cornered snag near the hem. If Mama saw it she'd make me spend a half day getting the patch to suit her. Mama thinks patches ought to be every bit as nice as embroidery-work. I just wasn't of a mind to patch today so I lifted our cornshuck mattress to slip the petticoat under it and do it some other time.

Between the bed cords and the frame I saw a corner of pink paper. It was the one Nell showed me when I had the measles. It was like a shove in the back.

I'd advertise in that paper for a wife for Tyler!

I read all the letters first. It seemed kind of odd that those folks had to get help because they all described themselves as good prospects. I know there were lots of letters from girls that sounded as if they'd make a better wife for Tyler than Miss Charity.

I don't want to knock Miss Charity, but she wasn't any great hand with the skillet—and Tyler loved to eat. And it was real important to her how a person spelled or conjugated a verb or bounded the states. Tyler was no great shakes at such things, and it might make her very unhappy. Why, come to think of it, I was doing them both a favor.

With all the practice I'd had writing my book, a letter shouldn't be too hard. This one was. Took me more than an hour. Four sheets of the tablet paper Gran'ma Murdock sent. And I gnawed a quarter-inch off my pen staff.

After reading those fancy-sounding letters I hated to come out and say that Tyler was a big, awkward, red-headed, freckled-faced cowhand. And poor as an orphan dogie besides. I had a time making it sound right.

"Want to hear from young lady who is good cook and fairly pretty—" I put it "fairly" because we didn't want any stuck-up neighbors. "Am owner of fine claim in Cherokee Strip where air is best in the world. Good prospects. Former cattleman. Do not wish to say I am handsome but will enclose picture for interested party to see. Can provide home—" I didn't say "dugout home" because people in the East have such funny ideas about us anyway— "and high-class refined neighbors. Write right now. *Tempus fugits.*"

That last is Latin. Gran'pa Murdock told me it means "Get a hustle on." I thought it added a refined touch.

Now, about the picture. It wouldn't be a good idea to send one of Tyler, even if I had one, which I didn't. I had a picture in mind to send, and it wouldn't do a bit of harm because the person in the picture was already married. I cat-footed into the parlor and got the album with the purple plush cover and slid the picture of Papa out from between the double page. It was taken at Abilene, Kansas, before he was married, and it was a real daisy. He had on a derby hat, kid gloves held careless-like in one hand, a striped suit, and a gold watch chain double-looped across his vest. In those days his moustache curled at the ends. He was leaning against a fern stand. Even if he is my father, it's a picture anybody would look at twice.

Getting the dollar to enclose was the next thing. I guess you know by now that I had no more chance of having a dollar than a frog has need of a shaving mug. But I knew what to do. Ask for credit.

Papa had said not a week before that he'd decided to ask Mr. Merton for credit. It went against the grain but he'd have to do it.

"That's fine," Mama had said. "How about a bolt of calico?"

"Nossir!" Papa smacked the table. "No folderols. Just grub, and as little of that as we can manage."

"All right," Mama said. "Whatever you say, Joe. Girls, no new dresses."

I could see Papa weaken. "Louise, you know I'd dress you and the girls in silk and satin and put you on a cushion to sew a fine seam if I could." He pulled at his moustache. "Well, one bolt of calico. That's a-l-l. And we'll pay Ed just as soon after harvest as we get paid."

So that's the way I ended the letter.

". . . I do not have a dollar right now to enclose so please give me credit. I will pay you right after harvest. Respectfully yrs . . ."

Then came the hard part. Signing Tyler's name. I knew it was bad to do that, but how could I do it any other way? Then I remembered what Gran'ma Murdock always said as she thumped us with her silver thimble when we misbehaved . . . "You'll live to thank me for this."

Tyler would live to thank me. I was pretty sure.

I addressed the letter and put it up on the clock shelf where we always put mail to go to Hardpan. I put it in between a poem that Nell was sending to the *Youth's Companion,* and a letter Tom had written to the W. W. Judy Co., Fur and Hides, St. Louis, Mo. Once it was out of my hands I felt better.

I patched my petticoat and didn't have to take it out but twice. I got out the speller and reviewed all the hard words so that Miss Charity could be proud of me when school started.

Maybe she'd live to thank me, too.

Then something happened that made me forget all about the letter. Gurdys pulled up stakes and left!

Mrs. Gurdy came over early in the morning. Her eyes were all red and her hair looked like it was combed with an egg whisk. She cried and cried and wiped her nose on the hem of her dress and cried some more.

I took Louise Betsy and bounced her on my shoulder. Mama got Mrs. Gurdy calmed down enough to talk.

"He won't stay no-place," she said. "This is the longest he's ever been anywheres. An' now he's pullin' out." She began to cry again. Louise Betsy patted my face with her soft little hand. I loved her so hard that to think about not seeing her made me blink to hold the tears back.

"I'm so sorry," Mama kept saying, over and over. "Isn't there anything I can do? I'll ask Joe to talk to Mr. Gurdy—"

"I've talked till I'm black in th' face. It won't do a livin' bit o' good to talk. The mister might get him settled down for a week—or a month—then he'd get itchy-footed and it'd all be to go through with again." She sighed. "It's just the way Whit is. Just the way."

"Where's he going?" Nell asked.

"Oh, he talks some about Texas. Some about Colorado. If you ask me, I don't think he knows . . ."

"Maybe he'll change his mind," I said.

"No, honey. He might change it as to whicha*way*, but he's got to *go*. But I just came over to say 'thanky' for all you've done. Lettin' Tom run with Garvery— don't think I don't know it was hard for you to do that."

Mama turned red in the face, but she didn't deny it.

"And askin' us to the house raisin'. Then Louise Betsy. . . . Why, I might've died without you, Miz Richardson. And if I had, who'd've done for Whit?"

It's hard to understand grown-ups. Here she was worrying about Mr. Gurdy—and after the way he'd acted.

"I thought for a little while he'd be different here. Givin' the land for the school; I figgered that might hold him—"

So she'd been the one that had thought of it!

"I thought next term I might get Garvery in school. That teacher seems like a nice lady. And I wanted Louise Betsy to have her chanct—" She sighed again and it was worse to hear than her crying. "But a man cain't go against hisself, and Whit was born to roam."

There didn't seem to be anything else to say. Mama kept telling her that we'd miss her and they'd been good neighbors and if they ever came back our way they were to be sure and stop. Mrs. Gurdy nodded and nodded and drank the coffee Nell heated up. Mama wrapped the slab of gingerbread she'd just baked—first flour we'd had on credit—and gave it to Mrs. Gurdy to take along. I asked for one of Louise Betsy's curls to keep. Mama got the scissors and clipped it off; Mrs. Gurdy said she couldn't trust her own hand.

After two or three tries at it Mrs. Gurdy got up to go. She gave us a bottle of the bait oil Garvery sent to Tom. Garvery wasn't much of a one for talking, she said, but he didn't want Tom to forget him. She said Mr. Gurdy wouldn't come with her because he hated to face up to Miz Richardson after all he'd promised the night Louise Betsy was born. And would we please tell the lady in Kansas that the baby clothes were beautiful, just beautiful?

Then she gulped and Mama was swallowing hard and Nell was blinking her eyes—but I was out-and-out crying and I didn't try to hide it. Mrs. Gurdy took Louise Betsy and the warm place where she'd been in my arms felt awful—just awful. And she walked out the door with Louise Betsy's brown curls bobbing over her shoulder.

Mama and Nell and I watched her out of sight.

"That man ought to be horsewhipped!" I doubled my fists.

"He ought to be boiled in oil!" Nell said.

"That wouldn't help any," Mama said. "He is what he is. At least she's found that out and she's not butting her head against a stone wall to change him."

"I'd butt down any stone wall—I'd—I'd—"

"You'd do wonders and eat cucumbers," Mama smiled kind of sad at me, "but when you love somebody—that makes a difference."

"Love *him?* That—that—" Nell and I both said it.

"Yes, loves him. That's the way things happen." Mama stopped and I thought she was going to give us a talking-to about being careful to marry the right person; instead she just smiled again. "You're both too young to understand."

It was the first time I'd ever been glad that I was "too young."

Chapter 9

Now we had come up to the time for harvest. What had been weeks or months before had melted away in the hot sun and it was days now, just days. Papa went to bargain with Mr. Brunner for his threshing outfit and came home shaking his head.

"Why'd you go to him?" Mama asked. "Penny-pinching—"

"Because he keeps his stuff in good shape. I don't want an outfit that'll break down and lose me a day's time fiddlin' with it."

"Well, you don't have to talk to *me* like that."

"Who's harvestin' this crop? You or me?"

That was the way it had been for days, now. Our whole family crosswise with each other. Every morning the sky was blue and the sun was bright and the crop was gold. But in an hour—or even a quarter of an hour—it could all change. Knowing that was like the game we play at parties, "Heavy, heavy hangs over thy head—" A money crop's a touchy thing in a family.

In the late afternoons the big thunderheads sailed up in the sky and piled together. Other times of the year I thought they were like beautiful fairy ships; now, I hated to look at them. They were part of the weather and the weather was a big black giant, holding all of us in the palm of his hand, making up his mind what to do.

When I told that to Mama she said it was downright sinful to feel that way and I was to read a chapter of the Bible as a punishment. I picked the 26th chapter of Numbers because I liked the long list of names and I read it out loud. Nell said for me to stop, for goodness' sakes, but I didn't. I kept right on till I came to, "Joshua, the son of Nun." I think that's funny, even if it is in the Bible.

Nell was trying to write a poem about a king that loved a beggar maid. I said if we didn't make this crop we'd be beggar maids ourselves. Nell said that in stories beggar maids usually turned out pretty well, but she couldn't stand to go back to Kansas to live and never see Thad again. I said she couldn't tell him from Shad, so what difference did it make? And she got her feelings hurt. Tom was sitting out on the back steps whittling at something; he wouldn't admit it for the world but he missed Garvery like a front tooth. At supper Mama had to go out in the yard and get Papa and she said would he *please* stop watching the sky and come and eat? Papa said that he'd stop if she would and wasn't this the third day the cornbread had been scorched? I guess you can see how it was at our house.

Next morning at breakfast things came to a head. Nell and Tom were kicking each other under the table and I was waiting for a chance to kick both of them. Papa pushed back his kaffir mush and said it turned his stomach. Mama stood up with her spoon in her hand and banged it on the table.

"I can't stand this any longer. We're acting like a bunch of wild Indians!"

"Never saw any Injuns get worked up over a crop," Tom grumbled.

"Young man—" Papa said to Tom, but Mama waved him off.

"He's right, Joe. Some ways they're smarter'n we are. Mr. Runninghorse came by yesterday and I asked about Mrs. Runninghorse and he said she'd taken the children to camp down on the creek and pick sand plums."

"Don't see why that makes 'em so smart. How'd you feel if I didn't put in a crop? Be like Gurdys an' move on?"

"Now Joe, I'm not going to argue. I've just got this to say. The whole family's strung up like a cheap fiddle. I say, let's take the day off and go plum picking."

"And take our dinner," Nell said.

"And go wading," I said at the same time.

"There's some big catfish in the potholes, Garvery said." Tom put in.

"By golly, it's been a long time since I wet a fish line," Papa said.

"I can see who's going to gather sand plums for jell!" Mama said.

We piled into the wagon, our dinner with us. Not a fancy picnic like back in Kansas with fried chicken, layer cake, and deviled eggs. We had stewed rabbit left from last night, cold cornbread—a little scorched— beans cooked down with you-know-what. Right at the last minute Papa came out carrying a big watermelon. We yelled and clapped just the way we would at a tent show. He put the big melon in the back of the wagon on the quilt, between Nell and me.

"Euchre'd Ed Brunner out of this when I went over to talk some more about his threshing outfit. Aimed to save it for Sunday, but I reckon it'll come in handy today."

We rode along singing; we didn't take turns today. We just sang whatever came into our heads and the one who sang the loudest pulled the others into his song. A roadrunner bobbed up ahead of us, his tail feathers bobbing.

"Wants a race," Tom said. "Thinks he's old Dan Patch."

"We'll give 'im a race." Papa shook the reins over the mustangs. They were always ready to run and the wagon began to rumble on their heels. Nell and I grabbed ahold of the sides.

"Joe! Be careful!" Mama called out. We knew she wasn't really scared, though, because if she'd been scared she wouldn't have said a word for fear of spooking the team.

"G'along. . . . Go git 'im. . . ." Papa stood up, waving the whip, just like the Roman Ride in *Ben Hur*.

"Yippee-ki-yay!"

"Ride 'em cowhand!"

"Up Salt Creek without a paddle!"

All of us were yelling and carrying on, bouncing on the quilts and . . . wham! The wagon hit a chuck hole. It lofted us about a foot into the air and we came down hard, all bunched up. Papa nearly toppled out but Mama caught his galluses.

"Whoa-up—whoa up— Steady—steady—whoa-up —easy—easy—" Papa talked the team down and got them to stand, quivering in the harness, their eyes rolling.

"Well, how'd you folks like the second Run in the Strip?"

Before Papa got an answer, Mama wailed, "Joe—look!"

Where that big green watermelon had been was empty space!

Papa didn't say one single word. He just clucked to the team, hauled on the reins, turned 'em on a circle tight as a dime with a nickel left for change. Back we went over the tracks we'd made. The dust wasn't even settled. There was the melon, right beside the chuckhole, busted into twenty pieces.

"Last one out's a dirty sooner!"

We hit the dirt together, grabbed up hunks of the melon and started eating. The juice was sugar-sweet, the red meat crisp and cool. I spit the seeds as I ate and I went right down to the white rind.

Mama and Nell got into a seed-squirting contest and Mama won. Papa told about the time he got shot at swiping melons when he was a boy and Mama didn't even put a moral on the story. Tom gave the mustangs each a hunk and they ate just the way we did, only not spitting out seeds.

We got down to the flats where the sand plums grow about an hour before noon.

Sand plums grow on short trees or tall bushes. They're a reddish yellow with a look around the stem as if smoke had settled on them . . . bluish smoke. You can't beat the jelly and preserves they make, if you have plenty of sugar. And if you don't—and we didn't—you can make plum leather. That means to cook up the plums, rub 'em through a colander, and spread the pulp out in pans to dry in the sun. When it gets dry and tough and leathery, roll it up in cheese cloth, then when you can buy sugar you can cook the "leather" into plum butter. In between times it's good to pinch off a chunk to chew on. Puckery, but good.

Each of us had a bucket or a pan and the plums went "plink-plink-plink." Then the plinking stopped and the buckets began to get so heavy that the bail cut into your hand. When the buckets were full—plumb full! —we dumped them onto the wagon sheet Papa had spread out on the ground.

At noon Tom made a fire. Mr. Runninghorse had taught him, "White man make big fire; cook him. Indian make little fire; cook meat." So ours was a little fire. Mama heated up the stew and the beans and we poured them on the scorched cornbread and it tasted five times as good as it would have at our house. We lolled around to settle our dinners till Mama said we'd had time to settle a turkey dinner, and how about picking some more plums? Papa said would she please re-

member that this was a pleasure trip and he proposed
to go fishing and to take Tom along. Tom had the
poles out of the wagon before you could say "Oklahoma Territory."

Mama laughed a little at the sight of the two of them,
walking off toward the creek, in perfect step. Then
she took up her bucket.

"I'm going to pick some more plums. If you want
to, come along."

The three of us worked close together in a patch
just oozing plums. Mama told us stories about when
she was a little girl. They are my favorite stories and I

wish Mama would write them down. She says that two writers in one family is enough. Maybe a little too much.

She told us about the two dolls with kid bodies and china heads that Gran'ma Murdock's sister, back in Massachusetts sent out to Kansas when Mama was six and her own sister, Aunt Mag, was eight. Those dolls came all the way, by steam cars, baggage wagons, river-boats, and got there in perfect shape. They were all dressed up in fancy taffeta dresses trimmed with beads and they had tiny lace mitts and bonnets with ostrich feathers—they were lots fancier than any dolls we could imagine, even nicer than Miss Sophy Sophronia had been. They were just about the nicest dolls that had ever been in the Territory of Kansas.

"Then—" Mama always tells it this way, "then, the very first day I dropped my doll on her head and it broke into a hundred pieces."

"Tell about Aunt Mag." I said, "Tell what she did."

"Your Aunt Mag was a sweet unselfish sister. She never wanted to have anything more than I did, and she took her doll and dropped it, right in the same spot, on purpose. And of course it broke, too."

"I think that's wonderful," Nell said.

"I think it's crazy," I said.

"You're both right," Mama said. "But that was just the way your Aunt Mag was. I've never stopped missing her. Gone for twenty years and it's just as if it were yesterday—"

"What happened then?" Mama always got teary when she talked about Aunt Mag's dying of typhoid fever. "Tell about Gran'ma."

"Well, your Gran'ma put us to bed for the rest of the day and gave us nothing but bread and water. We thought we were the most put-upon two girls in the whole world! The next morning your Gran'ma came in and told us that it had been the worst day *she'd* ever spent. I didn't believe her then—they'd had chicken and dumplings for supper and the smell had about been the death of me—but now I know what she meant." Mama patted my shoulder.

"Tell about the dolls," I said.

"My goodness, Betsy, you know all this better than I do. Well, your Gran'ma took the kid bodies of the dolls and she made heads out of stuffed stockings and embroidered faces on them and put shoe button eyes and black yard braids and we loved them better than any dolls we ever had. Now, let's get on with our plum picking."

"Please tell me some more," Nell said.

"Tell about the Bushwhackers and how they came and you had to hide in the barn and they took Gran'pa's horse and—"

"There's no use to keep going over those stories,"

Mama said. "The war's all over long ago. Let's not be the ones to keep it alive."

I knew she meant we weren't to talk about the Civil War on account of Rymans. All their folks were Confederates and both our grandfathers and six uncles fought in the Union Army.

"You said we'd go wading," I told her.

"I thought *you* said that," Mama poured her plums onto the wagon sheet. "Oh well, I expect that's a-plenty. Come along."

Wildcat Creek was the same creek that ran past the old Diamond, where the cattle forded. Up here it was narrow instead of wide. Nell and I took off our shoes and stockings and waded in, laughing at the way it felt so *cold* at first. Mama sat on the bank saying, "Be careful, girls. . . . Hold your skirts up high. . . . Be careful. . . . There might be water moccasins around that brush . . . . Don't step in a pothole. . . ."

In the shallow places minnows darted around like tiny arrows. Baby crawdads backed through the soft mud. The water felt warm enough now, except for the hem of my skirt that was sopping wet and flapped against my bare legs. Nell waded on upstream. I found a chipped stone piece and Mama said maybe it was an arrowhead and weren't we ready to come out. I said no, we were just good started and why didn't she come in?

"Me? Go wading? It's been many a long day. . . .
But I don't know why not. There's nobody around to
see."

Mama took off her shoes and peeled off her long
black cotton stockings and hitched up her skirts and
came in with me, giggling just the way Nell and I had.

Nell came back with some bleached crawdad claws. Her eyes got as big as saucers.

"Mama! Forevermore!"

"Betsy told me to," Mama laughed. "Let's go up-stream."

We waded along, slipping and sliding and grabbing each other and having more fun than a barrel of monkeys. It was deep and narrow and we had to hold our skirts 'way up and we didn't even notice that we were getting close to the place where the road to Hardpan crossed the creek. Then Mama looked up. In a horrified voice she said, "Girls! Drop your skirts!"

A buggy was standing there, and a man driving. We all three dropped our skirts at once. They made a little sighing sound as they ballooned out and hit the water. Mama's face was a sight to behold!

The man leaned out of the buggy and called, "Howdy, Louise. I thought you folks were Dry Land Methodists!"

"Ed Merton!" Mama said. "You gave me a real turn. Come on in, the water's fine."

"Some other time," Mr. Merton said. "I got a kind of a surprise package here for you folks. I was aimin' to deliver it to your house, but 'long as you're here—"

He didn't get anything more said, for, out of the buggy, where she'd been crouched down behind the dashboard, jumped—Miss Charity!

She came running toward us, and Mama and Nell and I went hurrying across the creek with our skirts dragging and our hands muddy and such a kissing and carrying on you never heard.

"I just couldn't stay away any longer," she said. "I hope you don't mind my coming back early. I said 'after harvest' . . . but there's a lot I can do to get ready and maybe I can help you with the cooking."

"Don't say another word," Mama hugged Miss Charity again. "You're as welcome as the flowers in May. Now tell me all the Kansas news."

"There's not much to tell. Everybody's fine. How's— how's everybody here? How's—Rymans?"

"Fine," Mama said. "The girls will be ready to start back to school just as soon as harvest is over and Shad and Thad—Nell has more news of them than I have."

Nell giggled like a silly. "Just of Thad."

"How are Gurdys? And Louise Betsy?"

"Why, Gurdys are gone. Just pulled up stakes and left." Mama frowned. "I'm sure I wrote you about that, Charity. How she came over to tell us goodbye, and how much we missed the baby."

"Don't, Mama," I said. Even now it hurt me to think that I'd never see Louise Betsy again, and she was my very own namesake.

"But I'm sure that I wrote—"

"I didn't get the letter," Miss Charity said, "but

now that I'm here you can tell me all about it some other time. Betsy, how's Warren?"

"Least said, soonest mended."

"I saw Tyler yesterday," Nell put in, sly as a pussy-cat. "He was out looking at the wheat crop."

"How is the wheat coming along around here?"

"Tyler and Joe, they've both got a good chance to make something," Mr. Merton said. "Barring rain, hail, wind, a drop in the market, and other accidents."

"Oh, hush," Mama said. "Talk like that comes cheap."

"Where is Joe, anyway? Off worrying about the crop?"

"He's gone fishing. I guess that shows he's not worrying."

About that time Papa and Tom came around the bend carrying a big string of fish. They were tickled to see Miss Charity, only of course they couldn't show it the way we did. Papa gave Mr. Merton half the fish and they stood and talked politics and crops.

"I hear they've got some prairie fires over Auguston way," Mr. Merton said. "Jim Putney said they could see 'em from his place."

"Bad time for prairie fires with the wheat ripe."

"Don't know of any *good* time for a prairie fire. I've seen 'em in Kansas. I tell you—"

"I know," Papa cut him off. "I lived there, too."

"Well, I better be gettin' back to the store or the missus'll rawhide me for loafin'. Just thought I'd bring you folks your surprise package."

He left with us thanking him for Miss Charity and him thanking us for the fish.

It was almost dark when we got home from the plum picking. I was sitting by Miss Charity with Nell on the other side. When I stood up to get the kinks out of my legs I saw, along the edge of the sky, a dull reddish light. Maybe it was the sunset. I stared at it, not wanting to know the truth.

"Joe," Mama said, "That red—over to the southwest . . . ."

"Yep," Papa nodded. "I been smellin' smoke quite some time."

"Why in the world didn't you say something?"

"Don't know as that would've done any good. Talkin' won't stop a prairie fire. Just hope and pray that the wind don't turn."

In the Strip the wind comes mostly from the south. It was that way now, a cool night wind that whispered in the leaves of the cottonwood tree. But if it swung around . . . . A southwest wind would catch us in the path of the prairie fire.

"How far off do you figger it is?" Tom asked.

"Four mile . . . . Five might be more like it. 'Bout

five mile." Papa climbed down from the wagon. Tom slid into the driver's seat.

"Don't put the team up yet," Papa said.

"Where are you going this time of night?" Mama asked.

"No place. I figger we'd better plow a fireguard around the house. Should've done it before now."

"With the fire five miles off?"

"Five mile isn't so far. If the wind turns—" Papa patted the near mustang on the nose. "Hate to work a team of mine by lantern light, old boy. It's a case of root hog or die, so we'd better root."

I honestly believe those wild, crazy mustangs understood every word. They didn't snort or buck or balk. They stood quiet while Tom hooked 'em up to the plow, as steady as Puss and Bess had ever been.

Chapter 10

*P*apa and Tom took turns at the plow. They turned up a wide strip of ground that took in the house, the soddy, the corral, and the well. Wide enough so that if the fire came close it wouldn't catch the house —maybe. The south wind held and that made the night cool but when the team passed where we stood, watching, I could see sweat on Papa's face by the light of the lantern. The smell of smoke was plain in the air; I wondered why I hadn't noticed it before.

"This is a sorry home-coming, Charity," Mama said.

"Don't say that, Cousin Louise! I'm glad I'm here. If anything happens to you folks, it happens to me."

She was a part of our family and nobody was going to take her away! I wanted to say it but I didn't know how.

"Maybe nothing will happen," Mama said. "But I think we'd better have some water on hand. Just in case—"

So all of us womenfolks went to the well with everything in the house that would hold water. I'll never forget the sound of the well rope, squeaking in the night. Or the way my hands felt from the rope burn. The red glow in the sky would die away and then it would climb back.

It was past midnight when Papa said we'd done all that could be done. In the morning, if things looked bad, he'd soak the shingles on the house.

"What about the wheat, Joe?" It was the question in all our minds but Mama was the one who came out with it.

Miss Charity, rubbing goose grease into her hands, stopped, dead still.

Papa pulled on his moustache. "I'm figgerin' on that little old dry-bed creek back of Tyler's holding the fire off the wheat. It'll do that, unless the wind swings southwest. If that happens—it's anybody's guess."

"Isn't there anything we can do?" Miss Charity asked.

"Not now. No time to plow a fireguard, the way it's strung out. If I hadn't gone fishin' today—"

"Don't blame yourself, Joe. That was my idea."

"No blame to anybody, Louise. We had a good day together and that's worth something." Papa patted Mama on the shoulder. "The way I figger—we'd better work toward saving the house. We've got to have a roof over our heads. Money we can live without—we've had plenty of practice at that."

"Will Tyler be all right?" Miss Charity looked worried.

"Sure. That dang dugout's fireproof. As for his crop. . . . Time'll tell, Charity. That's all I can say. Now—the whole caboodle of you go get some rest. You'll need it tomorrow. And pray that the wind don't turn." Papa walked off leading the lathered mustangs.

There are times when it's good to have somebody tell you just what to do, if it's somebody like Papa. We did what he said. Nell stayed on her knees praying so long that Miss Charity went over and found her fast asleep. Together we got her onto the bed without even waking her up. Miss Charity and I stood at the upstairs window. The whole south quarter of the sky was red. No two ways about it, the fire was coming closer.

I rested my head against Miss Charity's arm.

"I'm glad you're here. I want you to stay. Always."

"We'll see," Miss Charity said. "If the wind—"

The wind! Everything rested on the wind. I thought about the big black giant of the weather, and all of us scrambling around in the palm of his hand. I thought about his fiery eyes and his cheeks puffed out, ready to blow and turn the wind. I shivered.

"Get into my bed," Miss Charity said. "That'll give Nell more room."

When morning did come it wasn't like a proper morning in the Strip. The sky was dull; the sun looked tarnished. Smoke in the air stung my eyes.

"Let's get up on the roof," Papa said to Tom. "You womenfolks h'ist water and we'll soak the shingles."

We filled the buckets, Tom hauled them up on a rope, and Papa crawled along the roof, pouring water. The shingles were old and dry, dry as buffalo bones. They soaked up the water, bucket after bucket. Mama was at the well when the water began to come up muddy. She called to Papa.

"Joe—the well. We're getting near to the bottom."

I saw Papa shut his eyes. Then he set his jaw tighter.

"Give 'er time to fill up. That's a good deep well; I dug it myself."

Mama walked up to the house. "Couldn't you come down and rest a little? I don't think you slept a wink last night."

"Couldn't rest if I did come down. I feel easier up here where I can see."

"What . . . what can you see?"

"Oh—smoke. Some flame."

"How close is it?"

"Don't know as I can say. If the wind don't turn— if it just stays straight south . . ."

"Joe, if the worst comes to the worst we can go back to the soddy."

"I got that figgered, Louise, but thanky just the same for sayin' it." Papa looked down from the roof at Mama and smiled. "I still say we'll be all right if the wind don't turn."

"I think I'll take Nell into the house to rest a little," Mama said to me. "She's about done in. And I want you to walk over to Tyler's place and be sure he's all right. Charity, you go along with her."

Isn't that the way with grown-ups? They won't say what they mean. Mama knew Miss Charity wanted to see Tyler worse than anything, but a nice young lady— especially a schoolteacher—can't go to see a young man by herself. Not even if a prairie fire's coming his way! So I got stuck with going along. And Mama *knew* how I felt about Tyler and Miss Charity. . . .

We started out, walking down the old cattle drive road that runs between our claim and Tyler's. The grass on either side was uneasy. It moved and crackled. Rabbits ran past. Prairie chickens. Quail. Prairie dogs. A six-foot blacksnake looped through the grass.

Miss Charity caught my arm. "Betsy! Look!"

A buck deer tore by within ten yards of us and never even knew we were there. A black flake of ash settled in the bare ground that was the road. Another one. I watched the drift of the ash. I put my finger into my mouth, wet it and held it up. I didn't need to. I knew —Miss Charity knew—the rabbits, the quail, the snake, the deer all knew. . . .

The wind had turned!

We broke into a run that brought us pounding up to Tyler's dugout. He was standing just outside the door, staring toward the southwest. He grabbed Miss Charity by the shoulders.

"What in tarnation are you doing here?"

She rared back, stiff as a poker, but she couldn't answer for being winded. So I spoke up for both of us.

"We're here—because Mama—sent us—" I puffed. "An' that's all— Now we've seen—you're all right— we'll go home. . . ."

"I never meant that," Tyler said. "Stop behavin' like a female, Betsy Boy. I just meant it's dangerous, you two, roamin' around."

"The wind—it's turned," Miss Charity said.

"I know. I been trying to figger what to do." He looked at Miss Charity. "I thought you'd gone for good."

"I came back to get ready for the next term of school."

"Don't look like there'll be any school. Or anything else."

"There will be a school," Miss Charity said, as cool as an ice chest. "I can speak for that. As for 'anything else'—I'm not the one to say."

They just stood, looking at each other.

"If we could get up on the ledge over the dugout we could see more," I said. Tyler boosted us up, then he went to the corral and saddled his horse and brought it over and tied it close to the door. He climbed up there and stood between us.

There was the wheat. It stood, golden and proud, and ready for harvest. The southwest wind rippled through it. Already there was black ash drifting in. It wasn't a big spread of wheat. Taken together, Tyler's and ours wouldn't have filled a corner of one of the big farms I've seen in Kansas. But it was a first crop and a first crop's special. There was something of Papa, and Tyler, too, down there in that tall yellow wheat.

"Never thought I'd care about a crop," Tyler said. " 'Cep'n to get cash money for it."

A black flake of ash blew against Miss Charity's cheek. She wiped it away and it smeared, a long wet smear.

I touched his arm. "Tyler—the fire's jumped the dry-bed creek."

"All right, pardner," Tyler nodded at me. "I guess that tells me what I've got to do." He turned around from me and took Miss Charity by the shoulders and looked down at her.

"I want you to understand, Charity. I'm gonna set fire to my wheat. It'll make a backfire—and maybe it'll save Joe's. With the road between for a fireguard, if I backfire mine, his oughta be safe. If I don't—well, we're both goners."

"Oh Tyler—" Miss Charity choked.

"I just wanted you to know why, honey," he said. "They've been awful good to me, and there's five of them."

"Tyler, you'd better not," I said. "I don't think Papa would want you to. I don't think—"

"It's the only way, pardner," Tyler said. But he wasn't looking at me. He was just looking at Miss Charity and she was looking at him and their eyes were shining through the drifting smoke.

"Go on, but be careful," Miss Charity said, "don't get hurt!"

"Now you two gals, get those feed sacks I've been

usin' for rugs. Wet 'em down, and stand in the road, and if fire jumps the road beat it out. If things get outa hand, run for the dugout. Understand?"

"Yessir" I said.

It was the second time I'd "sirred" Tyler.

Tyler scrambled down off the ledge over the dugout, got a rag, doused it with coal oil, knotted it to his lariat, untied his horse and jumped to the saddle. He loosened his coiled lariat, struck a match along the leg of his

jeans and lighted the rag on the end. Then he grinned, waved, yelled *"Yippee-i-ki-yay!"* dug the spurs into his horse, and took out!

At the far end of the stand of wheat Tyler unrolled the lariat, and rode through the ripe wheat yelling like a Comanche. The wheat blazed up behind him. The horse screamed and ran like he was loco'ed but Tyler rode him! He rode him through the field twice and the fire roared.

Miss Charity and I ran up and down with wet sacks,

beating out little flames, and Tyler came back to help us. The two fires raced toward each other. The prairie fire had the southwest wind at its back, but our fire had the thick-sown wheat to feed on. When they came together it was like two armies doing battle.

Then, quicker than I can tell, the roaring, blazing flames died down. The fire swept on around to the unplowed grass on Gurdys' claim. It would hit Wildcat Creek and stop there.

We stood in the road and stared. All that was left of Tyler's wheat was a black, smoking silence. And our wheat still waved, golden and untouched.

"Well—" Tyler said into the silence. "Quite a show there for awhile. 'Most as good as Dodge City on the Fourth of July."

He had his arms around Miss Charity and she was crying into his shirt. Their faces were black with soot and smoke and I guess mine was, too. But I wasn't thinking about how funny they looked or how funny I looked. I was thinking about how Tyler had fired his crop to save ours.

Mama says that nobody grows up steady and even, that we stand still and then jump ahead—or fall behind—in spurts and starts. I guess that's right. All of a sudden I felt ten years older. I knew Nell was right— I'd been acting like a baby.

"Tyler," I said, "I'm a gump! It's all right for you

to marry Miss Charity. It's—it's—a real good idea!"

"Betsy!" Miss Charity said.

"I 'preciate that, Betsy Boy," Tyler said, "but don't say you're a gump. I wouldn't have a gump for a pardner. Here come your folks."

Sure enough, Papa and Tom had seen the whole thing from the roof and they'd got out the team and wagon and come on the jump, with Mama and Nell bouncing in the back like a couple of beans in a locust pod. Papa hauled on the mustangs and got 'em stopped.

"You crazy coot!" Papa was slapping Tyler on the back. "But you sure did the only thing—the only thing—"

"Listen everybody!" I said, "Tyler and Miss Charity are going to get married. I think it's wonderful! I think it's—splendiferous!"

My whole family looked at me with their eyes bugged out. I always have trouble with folks not knowing that I've changed inside. It seems so—so—meechy to have to stop and explain that I've changed. I want 'em to *know*.

"Betsy, when will you learn to behave like a lady?" Mama said.

"Things'd get kind of dull that way, Miss Louise," Tyler said. "I sure wish we could—what Betsy Boy said —but with the crop gone . . . ."

"I think I have something to say about this," Miss

Charity stood up straight with her blue eyes snapping out of her black face. "I won't marry you or any other man till I'm asked, properly. And you've never asked me. Not one single time!"

Tyler's jaw dropped. "Why, Charity—I just figgered . . . ."

"You can just re-figger. Do you want me or don't you?"

Then that big awkward uppity Tyler took off his hat and his red hair looked bright and clean above his dirty face. He got down on one knee, right in the middle of the road.

"Charity, honey, I love you, will you marry me when I can make another crop. I mean as soon as—"

Miss Charity smiled through the black and grime and she looked as beautiful as she did dressed up for the box social. "I will and I won't," she said. "I will marry you and I won't wait!"

Right there, in front of all of us, she kissed him.

Mama began to sniff and hunt for her handkerchief and so did Nell. I didn't; I was tickled pink! Papa cleared his throat.

"Is this a wedding or a funeral?" he said. "Never know from the way womenfolks carry on."

"I'm so happy," Mama sniffed, "but how can they marry with the crop gone and—"

Papa looked scandalized. "You surely didn't think

for one livin' minute I'd let Tyler do what he did for
us without goin' halvers with him on our crop, did
you? Why I never had anything else in mind from the
time I saw what the crazy galoot was up to."

"Now Joe—" Tyler started out. Papa held up his
hand.

"And another thing. As a member of the school committee I figger it's up to me to ask yore intentions? You
will let Charity go on teaching at Skiprock School,
won't you? Be a pity when it's just good started to have
it all tore up."

"That's up to Charity," Tyler said. "It's all right
with me if that's what she wants."

"Of course it's what I want," Miss Charity said. "I
want to keep on as long as Betsy's there. It's so . . .
un-tiresome!"

"*Yippee!*" I yelled. "*Excelsior!*"

"Let's get on back to the house," Papa said. "I'm still
uneasy."

"Hurry up," Nell said; "I want to write a poem!"

All of us piled into the wagon. Tyler hitched his
horse on behind and rode with us, holding hands with
Miss Charity. There were white rings around his eyes
and with his black face he looked like a he-coon, grinning down from a tree. There wasn't a soul in that
wagon that didn't know we'd all be on short rations,

old clothes, and home-cobbled shoes before another crop, but not a one of us cared.

Nell started the singing with "Love's Old Sweet Song," and we sang all the way back to our house with the black ashes falling around us.

That's the way a book ought to end. You know, with everybody happy and big plans and all. I wish I could end mine there, but I promised at the first I'd tell all the truth and I guess I have to.

The night after the prairie fire there was still smoke in the air and still a red glow in the sky. It was hard to get to sleep and when I finally did I waked up with a terrible, terrible feeling. At first I thought our old cat, Sir Toby, was sitting on my chest. Then I remembered that Sir Toby died back in Kansas, before we ever came to the Strip. I struggled and struggled to get clear awake. I thought that I was having a dream that I had done something wicked. Then I did wake up, and it wasn't a dream at all. I had really and truly sent that letter with Tyler's name forged to it, so that he would marry somebody else.

Suppose at this very minute a lady was riding on a railroad train, coming closer to the Strip with every turn of the wheels, and she had Tyler's address and Papa's picture, and she was bringing the letter.

Words began to drift around in my head. Forgery . . . false witness . . . thief. . . .

I turned and twisted on the bed till Nell mumbled at me in her sleep. Why couldn't I be like Nell? Sweet and polite and good? I almost hated her; it was *easy* for Nell to be good.

I swung my feet over the edge of the bed and dug my toes into the rag rug I'd helped Gran'ma Murdock braid. What would *she* think of me for doing a thing like that?

And Tyler? What would he think? I could hear him calling me 'pardner,' I remembered how nice he'd been about all the other things . . . the grass snake, the box social, the sneeze powder. Anybody but a blind bat could see he was the right man for Miss Charity. And what had I done? Tyler was wrong! I was a *gump*, an awful gump.

Downstairs I could hear Papa snoring like a volcano. I tiptoed down the steps and through the dark smoky house to Mama's side of the bed.

"Mama," I whispered, "please wake up."

One of the nice things about Mama is that when you're in trouble she doesn't waste time asking questions. She came right out of her sleep, put her hand up to my forehead to see if I had fever, then she slid out of bed and put on her calico wrapper.

"Let's not disturb Papa. He's all worn out."

She took my hand and we both tiptoed out to the back steps and sat down. Mama put her arm around me.

"Now, Betsy, what's troubling you?"

I told her the whole thing, then I put my face down in her lap. She hadn't said a word but I knew she must be thinking those awful words . . . forger . . . liar . . . thief. Still, her hand went on stroking my hair.

"This is a serious thing, Betsy."

"Yes ma'am. I know it now. I didn't think—"

"That's no excuse. The Lord gave you brains; He expects you to use them."

"Yes ma'am." We sat quiet till I couldn't stand it. "What—what do you think will happen? Will some lady come? Will Tyler have to marry her?"

"Tyler certainly won't have to marry her," Mama said, "Tyler didn't send the letter. But suppose somebody *did* come. Clear from Chicago, or even further? How do you think *she'd* feel?"

I hadn't really thought about that part. The other person wasn't real. Just a line of printing on pink paper.

"You were trifling with other people's lives, Betsy. I want you to understand that. No matter if you are a little girl, that's what you were doing. And it's serious."

"Will I—will I have to tell Tyler?"

"I'm afraid you will."

"He'll hate me! And so will Miss Charity! They'll never want to see me again. Tyler won't let me be his pardner. Couldn't—couldn't you tell Tyler? And tell him I'm sorry."

"I will go with you to tell him," Mama's hand never stopped stroking my hair, "but you will have to do the telling. You wrote the letter."

"If you whipped me would it do as well? Not with a switch, with Papa's razor strop."

"I wouldn't do it and you are too big for punishment like that. No, honey, you'll have to take your medicine."

"Everybody'll hate me," I said. "Everybody."

"You know that's not true. I won't hate you. I love you and I always have and I always will. Now—"

"What are you two whispering about?" It was Papa. He'd come up right behind us and we hadn't heard him. "Haven't you had enough excitement for one day? How can a man sleep with all this sh-sh-sh-ing?"

"We didn't mean to wake you up, Joe, but Betsy, here— Go on and tell him, Betsy."

It was like pulling teeth to say it all again, and to Papa who was always so careful and bent over backwards to keep his word good. He sat down on the step beside Mama.

"So you sent this letter? How about the money?"

"Oh, I asked for credit. I said that I'd pay . . . Tyler'd pay . . . right after harvest. That's the way you did with Mr. Merton. I thought it was all right."

"Hmmmm," Papa pulled on his moustache. "It is all right if you've got credit with a man, but I've got a feeling those folks are a strictly cash on the barrelhead outfit. When did you mail this letter?"

"I—I put it on the clock shelf for you to mail the way we always do. I didn't have a stamp but I knew you always got them."

Even in the dark I could feel Papa turn around and look at me. For a long time he just sat there, then he got up and went in the house. I felt worse than ever. I'd been so bad that Papa couldn't even bring himself to speak to me. Mama patted my arm.

"It's always darkest just before dawn, Betsy. Look over there in the east." Sure enough, it did seem the least bit lighter over there.

Papa came back then with the kitchen lamp lighted. He sat down on the step and he still didn't speak. I put my hands over my face because I couldn't bear to look at him.

"Well, it looks like this is the night for gettin' things off your chest," Papa said. My hands dropped and I blinked. It wasn't what I expected.

"What on earth are you talking about?" Mama said.

"That letter of Betsy's—those other letters up there on the clock shelf—I—I didn't mail 'em. I just didn't have the money to buy stamps and I didn't think I ought to ask Ed Merton for credit for that—the gover'-

ment makes him pay cash—so I just— Well, Louise, I just stuck the letters behind the clock. Been doin' it for weeks. Here."

He dropped a little pile of letters into Mama's lap. Nell's to the *Youth Companion,* Tom's to W. W. Judy, Fur and Hides, Mama's to Cousin Gertrude about her new baby, Mama's to Miss Charity. And mine! I'd never been so glad to see anything in my life! I snatched it up and I would have torn it into a million pieces but Mama put her hand over mine.

"Joe, why didn't you just tell me? I never thought—"

"I know," Papa said, "but I felt so *ornery* about it. A man that can't even buy stamps for his family is a sorry kind of a man."

"Joseph Thomas Richardson! You're the finest man in the Cherokee Strip! What difference does a little money make? I'm ashamed of you for even thinking it did."

"Well, I was goin' to mail 'em after harvest," Papa looked at me and kind of grinned. "I guess Betsy'n me, we figger alike."

"Oh Papa—Mama—I'm so glad. I mean, I'm so sorry." Well, it was the truth. I was both at the same time.

"I hope this has taught you a lesson," Mama said.

"Yes ma'am," I said. "Do you—do you still think I ought to go tell Tyler?"

"We-ell—" Mama balanced the letter on her finger-
tips.

"I'd say 'no,' " Papa said. "This is a time when
'least said, soonest mended' really means something.
And besides, Louise, I feel grateful myself for gettin'
out of a bind." He looked out at the burned-over
countryside. "Better get some sleep. Have to see Brunner about his threshing outfit for sure now."

But he didn't get up and go in. Instead he just sat.
All three of us just sat. I was glad to be quiet, and thank-
fulness filled me from the crown of my head to the tips
of my toes. The east grew lighter.

"How about that picture of Tyler?" Papa said.

"Not Tyler. He's awful nice but he is homely.
Honestly he is. I wanted somebody real handsome so
I—I sent your picture, Papa."

"My picture?" Papa's face turned red in the lamp
light.

"I don't know anybody in these parts that's handsomer than you are," Mama said.

"I'll be dogged. I'll be *double-dogged!*"

Mama tore open the envelope and the picture fell
out. They put their heads together, looking at it.

"Changed some since then," Papa said.

"You haven't changed so much." Mama rubbed her
cheek against Papa's. I could hear the bristle of his
whiskers. "You haven't changed at all."

"Neither have you," Papa said. "When I met you, you were the prettiest girl in Kansas. Now you're the prettiest one in Oklahoma Territory."

They weren't paying any attention to me. I don't think they even knew when I got up and went in the house. All at once I was terribly sleepy and my very own bed seemed like a wonderful place. I stumbled up the stairs and fell in beside Nell and curled around her.

It was just as if I'd been running a long ways and finally got home.

P.S. I guess it's all right to put a P.S. on a book. Anyway, I'm going to. I got to be in the wedding! Tyler said he wanted me for "best man" and I stood up with him. Gran'ma Murdock sent a pink dotted Swiss dress and Mama rolled my hair up on rags and made curls.

Warren Espey told me that I looked pretty. He told me twice so I know I heard it right the first time. I don't think he's near as crazy as I used to. Honestly, he's real nice.

The wedding was in the schoolhouse. If that sounds funny just go on and laugh. We didn't think it was funny. We thought it was wonderful because every last person in Skiprock School was tickled pink that Miss Charity had come to stay!

About the Author

Alberta Wilson Constant was born in Dalhart, Texas, but she spent her school years in Oklahoma and was graduated from Oklahoma City University.

Mrs. Constant remembers her grandfather's telling about taking part in the Run of '93, and about his later experiences on a homestead in the Kickapoo country. These stories sparked an interest that led to the writing of her first book, *Oklahoma Run.* Though this was an adult book, young people read it and then wrote to Mrs. Constant. They wanted to know about "the early days" in the Territory, so we have *Miss Charity Comes to Stay.*

Mrs. Constant is a versatile writer. She has written short stories and articles for some of our leading magazines. And in 1956 the conductor of the Oklahoma City Symphony, Guy Fraser Harrison, commissioned her to write the text of narration for Jack Frederick Kilpatrick's "Oklahoma Symphony." It was performed in 1957 as a part of Oklahoma's Centennial celebration.

Mrs. Constant, with her husband and two children, lives in Independence, Missouri.